FLYING THROUGH THE ASHES

BEVERLEY DOWLING

◆ **FriesenPress**

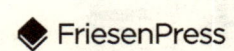

One Printers Way
Altona, MB R0G 0B0
Canada

www.friesenpress.com

Copyright © 2022 by Beverley Dowling
First Edition — 2022

All rights reserved.

No part of this publication may be reproduced in any form, or by any means, electronic or mechanical, including photocopying, recording, or any information browsing, storage, or retrieval system, without permission in writing from FriesenPress.

Although it contains many references to historic events, this is a work of fiction. The story of Edith and Harald, however, is real, and this book is dedicated to them.

ISBN
978-1-03-913078-4 (Hardcover)
978-1-03-913077-7 (Paperback)
978-1-03-913079-1 (Book)

1. FICTION, HISTORICAL, WORLD WAR II

Distributed to the trade by The Ingram Book Company

PART ONE
EDITH

LONDON, AUGUST 1936

The Rose and Crown was full, with the usual crowd doing the usual things. Margie Denning was allowing Harry Cummings to win at darts, as she nearly always did. She had set her hair and worn her floral frock, knowing that Harry would be at the pub and would want to play darts.

Millie Thompson played her usual repertoire at the piano and had gathered a crowd around it, singing "Roll Out the Barrel" and "Barbara Allen." Mr. Jones, the landlord of the pub, favoured "Knees Up Mother Brown" and danced to it behind the bar whenever he heard it.

The men at the corner table argued about the Olympics. They were friends, but their divergent views were strong.

"Bloody Berlin!" Mr. Carson shook his fist. "They'll be lettin' old Adolf lord it over all them athletes from all over the world! The Nazis won't keep our boys safe. They should've given it to Barcelona; Spain would've done the Olympics proud!" He shook his fist again, as though in a salute to Spain and anger at Germany.

"Aye," Mr. Griffin calmly flicked his cigarette, "but there's fightin' in Spain. They'd not be safe there either."

A few other patrons wanted to join in the discussion, but most kept singing while Millie played. Mr. Jones sang with the others while pulling pints. He stopped singing when a teenager pushed open the door.

"Well, if it isn't our Edie! Now, what might you be doin' 'ere, lass?"

"I'm buying my first pint."

Mr. Jones frowned at her. Edith Edwards was born on his street, and he had watched her grow up. She was petite and he knew she was older than she looked, but he was concerned. She was growing out of being a pretty little girl and into something more. Any girl would want a face like that, especially with her blonde curls; she would attract the lads, but a pretty face around her age could lead to dangers.

He understood how hard it had been for Edith and her brother, Peter, when their mum died. Their father spent too much time and money in the pub, as well as in other pubs where he was less well known. It was a relief when he remarried, to a kind woman who took Edith and Peter under her wing. Even so, with two new babies, Pat and Jimmy, there was little time for even the best-intentioned stepmother to watch over a spirited girl like Edith.

Mr. Jones repeated his question, "What might you be doin' 'ere, lass?"

"I told you. I'm buying my first pint."

"Now, lass, yer mum wouldna like it. Yer still just a bit too young."

"Anne's not my mum. She's my stepmum. My mum's long dead, and Dad wouldn't care."

"Now, Edie . . ."

"It's my life now. Will you pull my first pint, or do I have to go to the Boar's Head?"

Mr. Jones hesitated. His hesitation was the opening for comments from the crowd.

Margie Denning waited a moment until Harry Cummings shouted, "Come on, then, a pint for the lass!" Then Margie shouted, "Yes, give 'er the pint."

Millie Thompson, at the piano, stopped playing, smiled and said, "Yes, she's grown up. Let the lass join us."

The other people in the Rose and Crown smiled at Edie and urged Mr. Jones to relent: "Come on, she's a big girl now." "Always a first time." "We'll all take care of our Edie."

"Tell me, Edie," Mr. Jones hesitated, "'ave you ever 'ad a pint before?"

"Only stealing my dad's. You'll not tell?"

The people in the pub laughed and swore they would not tell.

"Well, I suppose so then. . . . Sooner or later . . ." Mr. Jones relented and was just about to pull the pint when he looked up and saw his son racing toward the pub.

Terry Jones dashed in, panting while trying to get words out. "Dad! He's done it! The black yank's done it!"

"Done what, lad?"

"Won the Olympics! Again! Best runner in the world! He showed old Adolf!"

Cheers went up in the pub. "A pint all 'round," someone shouted, while patrons banged the tables or clapped their hands.

"Yes, and 'ere's to that black yank!" shouted a man in the corner.

Mr. Jones pulled the pints, gave one to Edith, took one for himself, and raised it in honour of the victor. "To the yank!"

"The yank!"

Edith, along with everyone else in the Rose and Crown, raised a pint to the yank.

RURAL NORWAY
August 1936

Harald remained still and silent while Far studied the board. Far had taught him chess when he was a child, and in the early days, he realized that Far had allowed him to win. When he realized that he became determined to play the game seriously and practise with better players. Far was surprised but proud the first time his young son checkmated him. Harald was no longer a child, and chess had become a game they played as equals.

They both saw it as a war game, but it gave them pleasure, sitting at the table in front of their house, listening to the birds and the leaves rustling in the breeze. Sigvald and Elsa, the twins, were born a few years after Harald. Mor had wanted another child after her oldest but had had to wait. When the twins arrived, she thought they would complete her family, but Magda surprised her a few years later. The twins were old enough to walk to the village, so Mor sent them on occasional errands. She had to deal with running her home, as well as watching little Magda.

Sigvald and Elsa were on an errand and Magda was watching Mor bake while Harald and Far played chess outside, enjoying the sun and the clean air as much as the game itself. They saw Sigvald and Elsa running back to the house at the same time Magda ran out to them, and Mor came out of the house, her face shining with a smile, breathless even though she was just a few feet from her kitchen.

Far was reaching for his king's knight when Magda jumped up and knocked his arm.

"Far, the black American!" Magda jumped up and knocked him again.

Sigvald and Elsa arrived as Mor came toward the chess table.

"What?" Far asked while he and Harald both smiled, anticipating the news.

"Another gold medal?" Harald asked.

Mor, Sigvald, and Elsa nodded in unison as Magda jumped and twirled on the grass.

"Well, then." Far raised his beer stein in a salute to the American.

BAVARIA
August 1936

Konrad and Marta Meier heard the news about Jesse Owens at the same time as the people in the Rose and Crown and shortly before the family in Norway. The people in their village were proud of Germany, and almost all were proud of the leadership given by the Fuehrer. Marta wore the symbols of his party on her clothing and put flags in their largest window.

Konrad tended to remain silent whenever she praised the Fuehrer. Marta noticed a slight smile on his face when he heard the news about Jesse Owens, a man of an inferior race and from a mongrel country, winning glory in the Berlin Olympics. The hint of a smile infuriated Marta, but she could not admit it to her husband, or even to herself. Something as small as his smile was minor, but the triumph of Jesse Owens was large. She pounded, rather than kneaded, the bread dough she was working on. Then she picked it up and slapped it down on the board.

"You are such a fool, Konrad, for so many things, and now this! You cannot admire such a man! He is a great embarrassment. Our Aryan people should win those medals. We are the master race, and we cannot be happy about this."

"He is an embarrassment to us, perhaps, but I would like to meet him." He said it under his breath, anticipating her reaction.

"Meet him?" Her face became red. "Do not be ridiculous!"

She paused from speaking to punch the dough again. The punches were harder than usual, and she used the dough as the victim of her anger.

"And you!" She continued to punch the dough. "You are the other great embarrassment." She punched more vigorously, the dough now a stand-in for her husband. "You had a good job. Being the village policeman was a position of pride. Now you are nothing."

Konrad sat in his own silence and personal shame; he looked away from her.

"You are a fool, Konrad," Marta said. "You think you know better than the Fuehrer! Simple, silly man!"

There was nothing Konrad could say to his wife. He put on his jacket and cap and went out to the garden shed. There, he could have some peace. He had become bitter about the events of the past few years, and she had become bitter toward him. Their lives had changed, even though life in their village had seemed unchangeable. By 1936, the shock of the changes was over and the bitterness grew stronger.

The last war, led by the Kaiser against his cousin, the English king, took many men from the village, and the humiliation of the Treaty of Versailles was a sore point for all Germans, especially after the cruelty of conflict. Konrad had seen the pain in the eyes of his neighbours, the Satz family, when their oldest son was killed. Their uncle had been decorated for bravery, but their pride in him could not erase the grief they felt for their son. Konrad knew the loyalty the Satz family had shown to Germany and did not understand why they had become outcasts.

Jews and Lutherans had lived together in their area for many years, and he saw the Satz family and old Mrs. Leipzig and her pretty daughter as his neighbours. The Fuehrer, and Marta, now saw them as enemies for reasons Konrad could not understand. There was a different mood, one of unhappiness and fear. Marta followed the Fuehrer, but Konrad could not.

The garden shed was his place of sanctuary from Marta and her sharp tongue. There he could clean the rakes and sort the pots in privacy, away from his wife and from the people of the village. He knew they talked about him and his strange ways. Most men his age had sons in military service and were performing patriotic duties themselves, so they had no sympathy for anyone whose loyalty could be questioned.

A few years earlier, Konrad had become the village policeman. It was a good job, quiet and comfortable, and he was respected. Of course, there had been a few challenges. There was a housebreaking, which was easily solved, and the theft of an old painting, which was not, but the greatest challenge was control of his own weight.

Frau Donner routinely added cream to the hot chocolate she gave him in winter. Frau Mueller always insisted that he stop for a sausage. Frau Mueller made them herself and felt joy at the pleasure they gave Konrad. There were also pastries, fruit, and a beer or two, maybe more, to be consumed each day. He knew the villagers and shared their times of joy and grief, and they knew him. Children used to come up to him in the street, wanting to see his baton, knowing that he had treats for them.

Some of the older boys worried their parents by getting into mischief. Konrad understood and remembered his own youth. Heinrich Reiber and Johannes Dortmund, both basically nice boys, were his most frequent contacts. He could not show his amusement when dealing with them, even though he would always smile later, after he had chatted with their parents.

"You must teach your son to respect the property of others," he said, time after time, to the parents. "If he wants apples, he can ask for them. It is frightening to see someone climbing over a fence and climbing a tree. What if Fraulein Leipzig had been changing her clothing?"

The parents understood the concern, but Konrad knew how much Heinrich and Johannes would have enjoyed the view from the tree.

One boy, Hannes Kaufmann, stayed apart from the others. He did not climb fences and steal apples, but Konrad had become concerned when Fraulein Leipzig's cat was found hanging from a branch, the shoelace around its neck very much like the ones Hannes Kaufmann had worn on his old boots.

After Herr Hitler and his party became powerful, Hannes Kaufmann joined the Brownshirts. Konrad wanted to arrest him when he threw a brick through the window of the Satz family while they were eating their Friday Sabbath dinner.

"Why would you arrest Hannes Kaufmann?" Marta demanded.

"He threw a brick through the window of the Satz house while they were eating the family dinner. Someone could have been killed . . . and he strangled Fraulein Leipzig's cat. He frightens me."

"Who cares?" Marta screamed.

"I do."

"You care about a cat and a few Jews?"

"Yes, even the cat." He had spoken to himself, more than to Marta, and realized that concern about a cat seemed strange. Even he was surprised that he cared so deeply. He sensed that an attack on a helpless kitten could lead to other things, and the possibilities chilled him.

Hannes Kaufmann had shown no remorse when Konrad arrested him. It was at his home, and his parents were smiling, as though proud of their son.

"What if that brick had killed someone?" he asked, unable to understand why they would smile.

"What of it? No, old man, you should not arrest me. We are near the day when it will be me who arrests you." The boy, and his parents, sneered.

The threat of arrest was bravado at the time, but a week later, Konrad was unemployed and Hannes Kaufmann had taken his place. Konrad had not shown the right attitude toward the new leaders, and Hannes Kaufmann had shown his loyalty to them by following their suggestions as though they were orders. He was happy to throw rocks, whether into the houses of Jews or at them when they walked on the streets.

In 1935, a judge ruled that the police were not answerable to judges. In 1936, that ruling was solidified into written law. That was when the masters of the Reich considered other kinds of police duties. They announced the creation of a new force, which would work without uniforms and be invisible to the citizens while also being omnipresent. The new force was to be called the *Geheime Staatspolizei*, which would be shortened for common use to "Gestapo."

"They will be the finest police officers in the world!" Marta exclaimed when she heard the news. "You are too old to join, but you are not too old to help them, if only you would offer."

"They will not need my help." He had looked into his newspaper, avoiding Marta's eyes.

"You can offer."

"I cannot," Konrad said no more to her.

She tore the newspaper from his hands. "Why not? You are older than you were when you were a policeman, but all you have to do is offer. It is easy to see why they will not want you, but you can show your loyalty to the Reich and your love of Germany by offering to help. I do not understand why you will not do something so easy and so simple."

"This is not my Germany," he whispered.

She looked at him in anger. "You do not deserve this country. You worry about Jews and criminals and do nothing to help your country." She paused for a moment. "I despise you."

LONDON
September 3, 1939

Anne wanted the entire Edwards family to attend the Sunday services, but had no luck persuading Father. It was easy enough to make her own children, Pat and Jimmy, go along but she knew the older ones were reluctant.

Edith enjoyed the music but found the other parts of church services boring. Peter, who was only slightly younger, was even less enthusiastic, but they both went to keep Anne happy and to see the neighbours.

They liked Anne, even though they thought Father had married her a bit too soon after their mum died. When Pat and Jimmy were born, they enjoyed having a little sister and brother, despite new responsibilities. Father enjoyed it more than anyone else. Everyone had assumed that he was too old to have more children, so he liked the looks he got from the men at the pub after the little ones were born.

For Edith, going to church was a time to let the neighbours see her in attractive clothes, with her hair set and wearing bit of makeup. Father didn't approve of lipstick, but he didn't go to church, so she wore it with impunity. It made it harder for the ladies who washed the communion linens to clean them, but Edith was less concerned about them than about catching the eyes of the young men. She knew she would catch their eyes with or without lipstick and was aware of the comments from women—"Such pretty hair"—and from men—"Jolly bewitching, she is."

The family worried about Peter, knowing he was no longer a child and was approaching the age when he could be called up to fight.

There was fear about another war, and if they had one that dragged on as long as the last, he might be sent to the front. Pat and Jimmy had become more mischievous than usual, perhaps in reaction to tension in the family, and they were spending more time than usual with Peter, even though he discouraged their attention.

Two days earlier, Germany had invaded Poland. The family, even the children, were aware of what had happened in Europe. The authorities began the evacuation of city children to the countryside the day Poland was invaded. Even the children knew about Czechoslovakia, Austria, and now Poland. Hitler had been sending his troops out, in a widening circle, and seemed unstoppable. There had been both support for him and resistance to him in every invaded country.

Carrying on as usual seemed to be the only thing to do, despite the events going on in Europe and at the highest levels of diplomacy. The children were washed and dressed in their best clothes, and everyone else made an effort for a Sunday morning. It seemed more important than usual to look nice, as there was an underlying feeling that later Sundays might be different.

"This hat looks silly," Edith complained to Anne while studying herself in the upstairs hall mirror.

"No, it doesn't; it looks rather smart."

"I don't know why we have to wear hats at all! They're a lot of bother and they hide my hair." She pulled the hat down at another angle. "No, it hides my eyes this way. That won't do. Wait . . . maybe if I move it over a bit. I have to frame my face properly." She adjusted the hat again. "Oh no, that's worse! I shouldn't have bought this hat at all."

"What about your blue one?" Anne watched without moving, leaving her own hat as it was and trying to find a way to make Edith finish her adjustments.

"Right! Let me just change quickly!" She jumped away from the mirror and into her room.

"That dress you're wearing looks lovely," Anne called out to her, aware of how long a change of clothing could take.

"Yes, but it doesn't go with the blue hat," Edith called back while opening her wardrobe.

"You'll have to be quick about it. If you dawdle, we'll be late for church."

Peter waited at the bottom of the stairs with Pat and Jimmy. He knew what Edith's change of dress would mean.

"Mum! Just make her get cracking. We're going to be late again, and I'm always the one who has to manage these two." He pushed Jimmy away when the little boy tried to climb up for a piggy back ride.

Pat and Jimmy giggled and looked at each other in a way that meant they wanted to play tricks on Peter. Jimmy opened the door and called out, "Muffin! Muffin, come!"

"Oh no," Peter reacted. "Did you let the dog out? I suppose this means I'll have to go chasing it all over . . ."

Muffin, a tiny Yorkshire terrier, came toward Peter and stopped, with her paws forward, head down, and bottom up, eager for a treat. Peter was relieved to see the dog but anxious to get going.

"When will Edie be finished? I'm at my wits' end with these two, and now the dog as well!"

"I'm sure she'll be quick about it," Anne called down to her stepson, her voice more hopeful than certain.

When Pat looked toward the stairs, Jimmy pulled the ribbon from her hair.

"You did that!" Pat lunged toward her giggling little brother while her older brother held her back.

"Mum! It's getting urgent!" Peter held himself between Pat and Jimmy. "If Edie doesn't hurry, I'm leaving these two and going on my own."

"Edie!" Anne called. "Peter's right. Come along now."

Edith came out of her room, cheery and calm, in a fresh dress and the blue hat.

"There now, I wasn't all that long, was I?" Then she saw Pat and Jimmy. "Oh no! You two look rather the worse for wear! Peter, you didn't do a good job of handling them."

She smiled when she said it, leaving Peter exasperated. He started to open his mouth but stopped himself, as there was no point in arguing with Edith when he was angry and she was in that calm, all-knowing mood.

"Never mind that." Anne was anxious. "We've got to get going."

The children skipped down the front path and waited on the pavement for the others. Peter took charge of them while Anne and Edith walked out together.

"I don't know why we have to go to church at all," Edith complained.

"It's something we all do."

"Not Father."

"No, but there's no answering for him. That's not our problem."

"The vicar can be rather boring. You've said as much."

"Don't ever say that to anyone else. He's a kind man. Besides, it's a time for you to dress yourself up and look pretty, and I know you like chatting with the neighbours." Anne was anxious to get the family to church with as little rebellion as possible.

"I'd like a good long chat with that new lad down the road."

"Then we'd better get along, and you can stop being cheeky. You'll not be chatting with anyone if you go on with your dawdling."

St. Peter's was just at the corner of their road and they had a bit of time before the service. The vicar often had trouble getting the choirboys organized, so services rarely started on time. On any normal Sunday, with giggling choristers, there would be no problem about Edith taking a few minutes to change her clothes.

It was as usual, and Edith's timing didn't matter. The choir boys behaved as they, not the vicar, wanted. The family arrived just as the choir had gathered at the font by the west door.

"Ah, I see Terry Jones and Billy Lee are up to something," Anne whispered, smiling at Edith and Peter and nodding toward the culprits.

Terry Jones, slightly older than little Billy Lee, was giggling behind the vicar. Billy Lee stooped down while the vicar was distracted by another boy.

"Vicar, you'd better step lightly." Peter pointed to the vicar's shoes. The laces of left and right were neatly tied together.

"Oh no! Who did this?" the vicar asked while the boys giggled.

"It was me, sir," Billy Lee answered, holding his head down.

"It was, but I put him up to it," Terry Jones spoke up. "I'm the one to blame, sir."

"Well, you shouldn't do such things." The vicar smiled. "But you're a good lad for admitting it. You're both good lads. Now fix my shoes and let's get on."

Anne led her family to their places while the vicar led the choirboys in prayer. They had settled and were calm by the time the organist began the processional hymn.

It seemed to be an ordinary Sunday morning in St. Peter's, with the usual nodding hello to neighbours and watching young mothers try to control small children. The people held their prayer books and gave the responses in the liturgy, as they did every other Sunday. Everything fell into routine—until the end of Communion. The vicar was about the bless the congregation when a man entered and walked directly to him. The man handed the vicar a note, and the vicar turned pale. He paused before turning his face to the congregation.

"I have just received a note. As you all know, Germany invaded Poland two days ago. There has been a great deal of tension at the highest levels, and the results are not good. I am very sad to tell you that our country is now at war."

He paused, to give the congregation a chance to absorb the news. No one, not even the children, responded, so the vicar continued. "There will be terrible challenges, and each of us will be called upon to help, but for now, I invite you to kneel and join me in prayer."

Everyone moved in unison, all knees reaching the kneelers at the same moment, before all fell silent. No rustling of clothing, no giggles, no sighs of boredom, no quiet chatter. The vicar began the prayers, praying for safety for the souls and bodies of those gathered there and those in other places, praying for understanding and courage. Then he began the *Our Father* and everyone prayed in perfect unison. The congregation remained silent during the blessing and left the church quietly to return to their homes.

***

By the time the family returned home, Father was out, no doubt at the Rose and Crown. Anne knew what she had to do, as the plans had been made in advance.

"Right then, you two, go pick one thing each. They have to be small, as we'll not have space in the shelter for much."

Pat and Jimmy understood and went to get the things they had chosen. For Pat, it was her music box, with a little ballerina on top, and for Jimmy, it was his jack in the box, to frighten his mother and sister.

Anne led Edith through the house, room by room.

"We'll need blankets and extra pillows."

"Why extra?"

"They're bound to get damp."

"I'll never sleep in that thing."

"You jolly well will, my girl, and you'll be glad of the shelter."

"Will there really be bombs in this area?" Edith began to think about the coming reality.

"They can drop bombs anywhere they please," Anne answered kindly but needed to be firm about the truth. "And they won't be giving us notices in advance."

The Anderson shelter in the garden was ready. Anne had insisted that Father place it along the back fence, away from the house, to avoid the danger of part of the house crashing down on it. It had barely enough room for the family to sit, and the taller ones had to stay in the middle, where the roof curved up. The little ones had space at the sides. Father and Peter had covered the top with the earth that had been excavated to place the shelter, and Anne had planted peas on top in an effort to provide both camouflage and food.

"All these flowers will have to go." Anne was blunt. "We'll need the space in the garden for food, not flowers."

"I've always loved the scent of this rose." Edith bent toward her favourite.

"I do, too, love, but we need the space for marrows."

"Marrows are horrid."

"They won't seem so horrid when you're hungry. Come along now. Let's get those blankets into the shelter."

They used old wood to raise the blankets in an effort to avoid the dampness. Even while doing it, they understood the futility but felt they had to do it anyway.

"That new lad down the road told me about a dance tomorrow. You don't need me here, so I'll go."

"Really, Edie? Do you really think you should be going off to a dance the day after we go to war?"

"I don't see any bombs falling now, and it might be my last chance for goodness knows how long."

Anne knew she had to choose between knowing where Edith had gone and searching for her if she went off without telling. She relented.

"Be sure to take your gas mask and don't be late." She leaned forward to give Edith a hug. "You know how Father worries."

"I know you worry. You don't need to, though." Edith gave Anne a quick kiss. "You're right about the gas mask. I'll just pop inside and see where I left mine."

Anne raised her eyes to God, remembering the lectures about everyone needing to be aware of the location of gas masks and emergency equipment at all times.

The shock of the declaration of war was followed by expectation: everyone expected the bombs to fall immediately. Anne and Edith gathered the small things they could take if they had to leave their house. Food would be the top priority, but there were a few other things of special value.

"These were my mum's." Edith showed Anne two small copper dishes, barely large enough to hold a handful of pansies. "They're all I have of her."

Anne recognized the sadness and knew Edith had memories of her mother. She tried to be good to both stepchildren but understood that she was only a substitute for the mother they had lost. She took the dishes and patted Edith's hand. "Let's keep them in the Anderson, then; it's the best place."

Anderson shelters were distributed to people who had back gardens and, a bit later, Morrison shelters to those who did not. The Anderson shelter was corrugated metal and was designed to create an underground cave. Father had to dig into the earth to install it. The soil that was removed was set aside to cover the shelter, leaving damp soil both above and below.

"Room to grow vegetables on top," he decided.

They planted peas and marrows and cabbages and carrots. The government encouraged everyone to eat carrots as part of the war effort; improved night vision would be helpful during blackouts.

Anne had insisted that Edith and Peter continue to visit Aunty May. Aunt May had been angry when Father married Anne, for allowing another woman to take the place of her younger sister. When Anne ignored her harsh comments and continued to bring the children for visits, she realized how lucky her niece and nephew were to have Anne in their lives.

The visits went on, even when Anne was busy with two new babies, and Aunt May began to see them as another niece and nephew. Pat and Jimmy enjoyed the visits as much as Edith and Peter had at their age. Aunt May lived in a posh area and insisted that tea be served from a silver pot, with tiny sandwiches and something sweet, every afternoon.

When Edith took Pat to visit Aunt May, they drank tea in the front parlour, and then Pat was allowed to play house in the Morrison shelter. It had a steel top with wire mesh sides.

"Rather ugly thing in the house," Edith thought aloud.

"Oh, no matter, it's easy enough to just put on a table cloth and a vase of flowers."

"You seem so calm about everything," Edith looked at her aunt with admiration, "but aren't you worried that Bobbie could be called up?"

"Of course," Aunt May said while pouring the tea. "Every mother worries about the same thing."

"You sound ever so calm about it."

"We're English, dear. We have to sound calm even when we don't feel that way."

Edith noticed her glance toward the mantle, with its photos of her cousins as children and Uncle Harry in uniform when he went off to France in the last war.

NORWAY, AT THE SWEDISH BORDER
1940

Harald, blonde and blue-eyed like so many others, moved toward the cover of the woods. Nearly all the young men from his village were doing the same thing. The mothers had cried when their sons left, but they knew they had to go. It would have been dark if the sky had not been alive with the Northern Lights filling the sky with bold shades of green and blue and mauve, creating arcs and curves of brightness against darkness. The strong god-like creatures created by the Lights danced and played, as though intending to remind the human beings below of their smallness and weakness.

He paused, leaning on his ski poles, and looked up at the dancing Lights in the sky before looking toward the woods, with Sweden just a few miles beyond, and thinking back to the beginning of his journey.

"When did it begin?" he asked himself. There had been newsreels in the cinemas and announcements on the wireless, letting the people of Norway know what had happened in central Europe. Did this journey begin at the time of the putsch in a German beer hall? At the time Hitler became Fuehrer?

"Before I was born?" he wondered. Perhaps he had been predestined to ski toward the woods, his life set out even during the Great War and the meetings at Versailles.

"Silly thought," he said aloud. "Why do I even think such things?"

For this man, and for Norway, the change had come that April. There were rumours of King Haakon's flight from farm to farm, but details were unclear.

On the ninth of April, he had gotten up early to hunt and decided to stay out for the day. His mother still had torfisk, the dried cod from the previous year, but the family complained, wanting meat instead of fish. There were ducks on the open ponds and in the sky, and duck could be roasted over the fire.

He did well that day and came in with twelve fine birds tied over his shoulder. He felt pleased about his hunt but stopped whistling when he saw his sister running toward him. She was panting, her eyes were red and her braids were falling down, bouncing on her shoulders as she ran.

"Magda! What is it?" he asked, lifting her up and hugging her. "Why are you crying?"

"Oh, Harald! It's terrible! You must come . . . home . . . right now."

"What is it?"

"Ohhh, it's on the wireless . . . something terrible . . . Mor says you must come right now. . . . You must listen to the wireless."

The child cried against his shoulder as he carried her toward the house.

"It's all right, Magda . . . I'm here. . . Everything will be all right," he whispered, not wanting to upset her more by acknowledging the significance of an important announcement on the wireless.

He wanted to run toward the house but walked carefully, concerned about how Magda felt. He noticed that she had left the door partially open when she left and no one had taken a moment to close it, despite the chill of early April.

When he entered the house, he heard only the wireless. Mor and Far and Sigvald and Elsa were silent. Mor and Far looked older than they had just a few hours earlier. The words coming over the airwaves explained why.

Then Far turned toward him. "We've fallen."

"When?"

"Today. They've marched in and taken over. . . . It's the way it was everywhere else . . ."

"Not everywhere? France? England?"

"No. That can't be . . . at least not yet. . . . We can still get the BBC."

"What of the government?"

"That's Quisling," Mor replied.

"Who cares about Quisling? We're not fascists."

"No, but he's the puppet. You missed his broadcast," Far said.

"What did he say?"

"Oh, that's the shameful part. . . . He wants us to accept the troops . . . says we are part of the greater Germany and he is the only Norwegian who can govern. He says he's the prime minister!" Mor was angry.

"WHAT! That's treason!" Harald had never liked Vidkun Quisling, but he found it difficult to believe that one of his countrymen would do such a thing,

"The King won't go along with it. . . . He'll go into exile," Far predicted.

"Quisling wants us to join the SS," Sigvald said, holding his head high. "Men like you and me."

"Not you!" Mor responded. "You are too young, Sigvald. They'll leave you safe with us."

"I'm almost sixteen! I can shoot!"

"I can shoot, too," muttered Elsa, "but I'd shoot Quisling before anyone else."

"SHHHH." Far was looking at the wireless. "There's more. We must listen."

The family had tried to carry on as usual, but life in Norway had changed. The King fled from one farm to another, on the way to the sea, and joined his wife's family in London, where he was able to address his people over the BBC.

"Listening to our own king on a foreign wireless!" Elsa complained.

"Better than not hearing him at all," Far pointed out.

Vidkun Quisling, leader of the Norwegian fascist party, continued to tell the people to cease resistance and welcome the occupiers.

When couples went to the cinema, they saw newsreels glorifying the SS, asking Norwegian men to join. Some men from the village did leave to join the SS, but others made plans in whispers. People of all ages and genders joined the cells that would later form the Milorg, the Norwegian resistance. Many young men made another choice; that decision meant leaving the country.

"I have to go," Harald told his parents while the others were out of the house. "Not by sea . . . Albret and his brother told me not to do that."

"Why not?" asked Mor.

"The water is mined. . . . Some boats will get through, but Albret thinks Sweden is the better way out."

"Are you going with Albret?"

"No. We go alone, one man at a time, and by different routes. Albret has already started."

The sea to the west was unrealistic for most. Some boats did go to Scotland or England, but those boats were difficult to find and had to travel over mined water. For those closer to the border, the woods were the better way out. For them, the route to the west began with travel to the east, into Sweden, perhaps toward Russia, and then along whatever path might be found along the way. It couldn't be done in daylight, and by late April, the nightly darkness was becoming brief.

Harald thought back to the events of the previous few weeks: hunting game birds, comforting Magda, listening to the wireless, warning Sigvald and Elsa about how dangerous it would be for the family if they joined the resistance, and waxing his skis. Mor cried but hugged him and packed cheese and loaves of grovbrød. She had insisted on stuffing his pack with food.

He knew, as Mor did, that they might be hugging for the last time and that he had failed to persuade Sigvald and Elsa to avoid joining the Milorg. There was nothing he could do about them, but he had made his own choice. He pressed down on his ski poles and pushed toward the trees.

Harald approached the border under the cover of a snowstorm. It was unusual, as the weather should have been milder at that time of year. The strange weather was a comfort, as he wanted to be obscured, and his years of life in a rural area had given him skill on skis and an acute sense of direction. He pointed his skis toward the east and prayed. He understood that leaving on skis was his first challenge and crossing the border would be another. He knew there would be many challenges to follow but did not know how many. Finding the right people would be a constant priority—and one that allowed no mistakes.

Albret had made it sound easy, as though reaching an unoccupied neutral county would be a simple matter and would guarantee safety for the rest of his journey. He had always admired Albret for his attitude on life, but this would take more than mere optimism. Even in Sweden, there would be constant danger; it was officially neutral, but the Nazis had power and influence and could gather information from sympathizers.

He knew he would reach the village of Storaas, and he should look for the doctor and his wife, who would give him a meal and ale. The sky cleared, the snow settled, and he could see a village, hopefully Storaas, in the distance.

On nearing it, he realized that he had almost conquered his second challenge. He had entered Storaas when he fell and landed, semi-conscious, in the snow. Two days earlier, he had finished the food Mor had packed and had had very little sleep. Hunger and fatigue had become as challenging as any other part of the trip.

He was unaware of how much time had passed when he found himself in a bed in a warm room. A woman was holding a mug of steaming soup, watching a man examine his feet. Someone had removed Harald's clothing and covered him with a blanket.

"You are safe with us." The man smiled. "You may call me Arne, and this is my wife, Ebba."

Harald remained silent, waiting for an explanation.

"Drink this." The woman held the soup to his lips while the man held him up in a sitting position.

"Are those names real?" Harald asked.

"Why does it matter?" The man shrugged his shoulders. "I have examined you and you are strong."

"We opened your pack," Ebba said. "We wanted to know a bit more about you. I hope that does not offend you."

"No, I understand."

"Someone put this into the pack." She held up a dainty enamel bracelet made up of oval links, with a blue background and delicate painting on each of the many ovals. There were reindeer pulling a sleigh and tiny flowers, reminders of a Norwegian spring. "It is very beautiful."

"My mother must have put it in when she filled my pack with food." He took it from Ebba and stroked the delicate piece. "It was her favourite."

"Then it is for you to keep as a treasure and remember her love." Arne spoke quietly while Ebba studied the bracelet.

"We understand what you are doing." Ebba smiled. "One of your friends was here a few days ago. You have many more challenges, but you have passed the first two."

"The first two?"

"You have arrived in this village, and you have found us."

"Yes," Arne added, "but you must not stay long. Your friend will be waiting for you in Sweden."

"What happens there?"

"We have not been told. We will care for you briefly and send you on your way."

"With our blessings." Ebba touched his arm, as though she could place a blessing on him with her touch.

LONDON
1940

Anne always set the Sunday dining table with a lace cloth and her best dishes. Being at war was less intense than expected, as, so far, there had been no bombings and no immediate danger. People started calling it the phoney war. They carried gas masks and spent time in their shelters as a practise routine, but the calm after the declaration of war seemed anticlimactic. Even so, Anne sensed that change would come suddenly, and she wanted to carry on with her usual routine of a special meal on Sunday as long as possible.

The family sat at the table while Muffin remained on her cushion in the corner, head between her front paws, looking up at the family, ready to seize whatever small bits fell from their plates.

"Aren't we at war, Mummy?" Jimmy asked, while starting his treacle tart.

"We are. Why do you ask?"

"Shouldn't we be bombed?"

"We should not!"

"They're bringing in more rationing," Peter pointed out to his little brother. "You'll not be having all these lovely things."

When Peter dropped part of his biscuit, Muffin dashed forward.

"Now, we can't be having that!" Father insisted. "With rationing, we can't have food wasted on a dog."

"Don't be silly." Anne frowned. "Such a small dog eats very little, so we needn't be stingy."

"It's not just that." Father spoke in his tone of authority. "I've examined the government advice." He paused for attention. "If we get bombed or have to evacuate, animals will suffer terribly. The kindest thing is to put them out of their misery in advance."

Everyone at the table became silent.

"Dad, are you talking about Muffin?" Peter asked. "I'm not fond of the little blighter, but . . ."

"Yes, I am talking about Muffin. The government says a bolt gun is the fastest and kindest way to dispatch a pet. Right between the eyes. Mr. Carson has one, and I'll borrow it. He has to do the same thing for their Bruno." He looked around, hoping for support, but found none. "It's the only kind thing to do."

Father was surrounded by silence. He drew himself up in his most serious manner. The family remained still and silent until Anne spoke. "There's no need to be hasty." Her voice was calm and low. "We'll talk about this another time. Let's just enjoy our meal and play a few games later."

"Everyone needs to know the importance of rationing." Father spoke with grim authority again.

"Is that war?" Pat asked.

"That and more." Father responded. "Now eat up and let's not be silly. You'll be off to the countryside soon."

The table became silent. Anne held her body stiff for a moment.

"No." Anne spoke in a voice very different from the gentle tone she usually used.

"Are we going to a holiday camp?" Jimmy asked.

"It's war," Father cut into his pudding, "and we want to keep you safe, so it's off to the countryside for the little ones. There'll be no holiday for anyone."

"But the countryside is for holidays," Pat said.

"Let's not talk about this now." Anne glared at her husband.

"Why not? They have to know the truth. There'll be bombings, and I want them safe."

"Can Edie come?" Pat asked.

"No, she can't. Children only. Now go and wash up."

Pat and Jimmy left the table reluctantly, aware that the next discussion would be about them. The first question was from Peter.

"Does that include me, Father?"

"No, you're not a child. You're needed here."

Pat and Jimmy listened behind the door and knew exactly what expression their mother had on her face when she spoke.

"Why did you have to talk about that in front of them?"

"They have to go."

"No, they don't."

"I want what's best for them."

"As do I, but they're my children and I'll take care of them."

"And I'll help." Edith was angry at Father.

"As will I." Peter's comment ended the argument. "Aha! I see you silly things!" He smiled at the children, who were trying to hide behind the door.

"All right, you two," Father relented. "You don't have to go yet. We'll wait a bit, and then I'll decide when you go. Now, be off with you and wash up."

***

The children remained in London, and life seemed to go on as usual, despite the declaration of war. The children wore the same uniforms to school, with the gas mask being the only change. Father was secretly relieved that the children were at home. Having two little ones, along with all the all the other things she had to do, gave Anne little time to check on his own duties. He always let her know when he went out to tend the vegetable garden, but she noticed when he slipped off to the pub.

Father and Edith started going to the Rose and Crown together and played darts when the dart board was not being used by Margie Denning and Harry Cummings. Margie stopped allowing Harry to win, and he accepted his losses. The Rose and Crown was as busy as ever. Mr. Jones had pegs near the door for gas masks, and the shelter was just a few doors down the street, so the patrons' conversation went from war to other things and then back to war.

"Old Adolf thinks we're gonna let 'im and 'is blokes come on over and walk all over us."

"Not bloody likely."

"Not likely to welcome 'im over, but don't forget what's going on across the Channel."

"Right you are. We can't let down our guard."

"We can still get on with a few other things. Harry never takes me to see the new films." Margie hit her mark on the dart board. "That *Wizard of Oz* looked good and now it's over."

Mr. Jones spoke quietly. "My missus and I go mostly for the news reels."

The people in the pub fell silent. Newsboys cried the daily news, so anyone on the street was aware of the news before buying a paper but bought it anyway.

"We can still go to dances." Edith and all the other girls nodded.

Edith watched Hitler's rise and the news of invasions, but she continued to go dancing, showing off her legs by swirling her dress to the rhythm of swing music. She danced to swing, to the Jitterbug, and to the slow romantic sounds of "Moonlight Serenade."

While walking home from the dances, she would sing. The songs might be anything from "Three Little Fishes" to "We'll Hang Out the Washing on the Siegfried Line." Her favourite song was also Mr. Churchill's favourite. People sang it to the tune of the "Colonel Bogey March":

> *"Hitler has only got one ball,*
> *Goebbels has two but very small,*
> *Himmler is very sim'ler,*
> *And Goering has no balls at all."*

At first, the war seemed more like a theory than reality. There were drills and information meetings, but it seemed to be someone else's war. It didn't change the daily routines of walking in the park, watching cricket matches, or meeting friends.

That changed suddenly. The Battle of Britain began in July of 1940. In August of that year, the Luftwaffe began raids on British airfields and aircraft factories. On the twenty-third and twenty-fourth of August some of those pilots went off course and bombed London. The next day the RAF answered the bombing of London by bombing Berlin. A few days after that the blitz in London began in full force.

TORONTO
1940

After sitting up on the night train from New York, Harald's body ached from lack of sleep by the time he arrived at Union Station. He was low on cash and had not been able to buy a berth.

The autumn weather was chilly when he arrived in New York. The USA was still officially neutral, although the people there were concerned about how long neutrality could last. Americans were constantly reminded of the conflict in Europe and were aware that their neighbour to the north was at war. People at Grand Central Station saw the men, with Nordic clothing and strange accents, boarding trains for Canada, nearly all going to Toronto.

Harald was one of many men in patterned sweaters and stockings who boarded at Grand Central Station. The ticket agent didn't need to ask his destination, so there was no struggle with language and accents. His travels had exposed him to many languages, but the one he needed most was English. It was the language of New York and Toronto, and the one he would need in England.

The Norwegians on the train chatted and looked out the windows. Some things were similar to Norway, but New York State had a different landscape and the people wore different clothing. He did feel that Americans were being kind to the Norwegians and that they understood the reason for the trip.

Harold joined a few other young men, from areas he did not know, but all from Norway. They enjoyed the train ride from New York to Toronto. They had a destination, but while they were on the train, they could chat and learn about each other, and discover the ways of America. It was a relief to speak their native language, as all had struggled to learn English. They noticed a subtle change in accents and culture when they reached Union Station in Toronto.

"We have arrived," one said.

"Now what do we do?" asked another.

"Ask for directions?" responded a third.

The group went outside to the broad pavement in front of the station. Despite having a specific destination and feeling an urge to reach it, they seemed to be the only people who were not in a rush to go somewhere. Men in business suits hurried across the street. Women in smart dresses and hats went from one side to the other. Mothers gathered eager children, holding them back from the busy road.

Harold approached a man in a business suit. The man did not wait for a question before giving the answer.

"Just go down this street until you come to the lake. Turn right, and you'll see the planes. It's a bit of a walk, but you'll find it. Good luck to you." He tipped his hat, smiled, and crossed the street.

Harold and his group were saying thank you when the man disappeared into the crowd.

The man's directions seemed vague, but they were accurate and complete. As soon as Harald's group turned onto the street the man had indicated, they saw the lake. While they were walking toward it, they saw training planes flying above.

I'll be in one of those soon, thought Harald, knowing that each of his companions was thinking the same thing. Other thoughts crossed their minds, too. They wondered how long it would take to learn to fly, how safe the flying was, and how many of them would be shot down or captured. They let the thoughts flow through their minds, but no one spoke until they reached the road along the lake shore.

"Someone said Lakeshore Street, or Avenue, or Road, or something like that. Whatever it was, do you think this is it?" asked one.

"It must be. Look at the lake and the planes."

"They're coming from over there, west of us."

The others nodded, and the group walked west. The Canadian government had offered the airport on Toronto Island as a training base for Norwegians, for both the Royal Norwegian Air Force and the Norwegians who would fly with the British RAF. The airport was compact and efficient. The men were housed on the mainland, just across the narrow gap between the barracks area and the Island. The ferry from barracks to the airport was a simple raft.

Harold and his companions were tired after the train journey and their walk from the station, but they went directly to the recruitment office. They joined a line of young men, all in similar Nordic sweaters, no doubt knitted by their mothers.

"Your papers." The desk sergeant smiled directly at Harald.

It sounded like an order rather than a request, despite the smile. Harald handed him the documents in silence and watched while the sergeant examined them.

"Everything seems to be in order. Go over there for your medical, and they'll send you on to get your uniform. It's RAF. You'll be flying with a Norwegian squadron. Any questions?"

The sergeant gestured to the next man to come forward, before giving Harald time to ask questions or even checking to make sure he understood. There was no need for that. Whether or not the man had learned enough English to carry on a conversation, he knew where he was—and he had come there for the same reason as all the others.

LONDON
1941

"Army for me," Peter announced to the family while they were in the front room, with Father reading the newspaper and Anne knitting. Edith was modelling her new WAAF uniform. "They'll call me up for something," he continued, "and the army appeals more than the others."

"I hate to think of you going off to fight." Anne spoke in the quiet voice she used when worried, and continued to knit.

Edith had chosen the WAAF, over Father's objections, and enjoyed showing off the uniform.

"I don't know why you signed up for the WAAF." Father didn't like it at all.

"We all have to do something, and I didn't want to be a land girl."

"Those land girls keep us fed." Anne pointed out.

"They also dig dirt and muck manure."

"You'd be safer. You could get bombed in barracks," Father persisted.

"We could get bombed right here. That's why we have the shelter in the garden."

Father knew she enjoyed being in the WAAF and resigned himself to the thought that she did look nice in the uniform. It showed off her legs, and she did have nice legs.

Even though Edith and Peter were serving members of the military, they were stationed close enough to spend time at home when they had leaves. The family kept their routines as close as possible to those they had before the war.

Pat knew Edith's routine. Whenever she saw her sister with her hair in pin curls and wearing a silk dressing gown, it meant an evening out. The long blue chiffon dress with sparkly sequins was laid out on the bed, with the silver handbag and the soft blue evening wrap. There had been times when Edith had allowed her to try on the wrap, but never the dress. It was Edith's best one, and the only one still in good condition.

Pat had grown out of toddlerhood and had developed a fascination for her sister's feminine glamour. She watched the transformation before every dance. Edith would go into the bathroom, wearing a long satin wrap tied at the waist, carrying a tray of magic potions. It had creams, lotions, powders, pencils, brushes, and pots filled with mystery.

"Always wash your face," Edith told the child. "You'll get pimples if you don't."

There was no clear definition of a "pimple," but it sounded like something bad, so Pat took care to keep her face clean.

"Don't scrub too hard or you'll scrub off your skin."

It was confusing. There was obviously some perfect place between leaving dirt on a face and scrubbing off the skin.

On her clean face, Edith dabbed creams the same colour as her skin, then small smears of pink on her cheeks. She used a big fluffy thing to put powder all over for reasons unclear to Pat. There was a small box filled with a black substance. Edith would pick up a tiny stick with bristles at one end, lick the bristles, and then rub them over the black stuff and then over her eyelashes. The creams and powders dabbed on her eyelids were in various colours, but her lipstick was always red.

Once the face was perfect, Edith would brush her hair into the style she had chosen for the evening and pin it into place. Pat was allowed to follow her into her bedroom, where she replaced her dressing gown with a dress made for dancing. After that it was usually, "Isn't it a bit late?" then gently teasing the child with, "I'm off to a dance, but you're off to bed."

Pat understood the reasons for the dress and wrap, and for the pin curls and the glamour of the dressing gown, but one thing always baffled her and the explanation never made sense.

"What are you doing?" Pat leaned forward, almost touching Edith's legs.

"Drawing seams." She pushed her little sister back.

"Seams? What for?" Pat leaned forward again, getting as close to the line as she could.

"I can't get silk stockings. I've tried everywhere. No luck on the black market." She seemed sad.

"What market is black?"

"It's one where little girls go in and get terribly lost and all sorts of horrid things happen." Edith turned to Pat with a hard stare.

Pat paused, unsure whether Edith was teasing. "So why do you draw lines on your legs?"

"To make it look like I'm wearing silk stockings."

"Why?"

"You'll know when you're older," she smiled at the child, "For now, go ask Mummy."

"Why do you use a pencil?"

"It's all I have." She sounded sad again.

"Can I draw on my legs?"

"Yes, but not now."

"Why not?"

"Bit late, isn't it?" She couldn't explain the full reality to a child, so she gave her a hug and changed the topic. "Here we are—you've watched me do my face and you've watched me do my hair. You know what my dress looks like because you've seen me put it on again and again. . . . It's time for bed."

"Right now?"

"Here, one more hug and kiss and then off you go as soon as you get Peter. Is he ready?"

When Pat went down to the front parlour, she found Peter with his uniform brushed and his leather polished, clenching his fists and pacing the floor.

"She always does that! Always telling me to get ready when she'll likely take hours more. Go tell her I *am* ready and she *should* be."

Pat had watched the mysterious transformation of face and hair and lines drawn on legs, but there was nothing mysterious about Edith's way of dealing with her brother. He had to escort her to the dance. She used their father's wishes as her excuse, but if Peter was unavailable, she went dancing anyway, with or without a male companion.

"Why do I have to do this?" he would routinely ask.

"You know what Father's like. Just do as I say.".

***

"Oh, do stop complaining," Edith told him when they were on the bus. "I always make sure we get off at a good time."

They left the bus and joined a group of young people waiting at the ticket booth for the dance hall.

"Why do you always drag me along?" Peter complained.

"You know the routine. You don't have to stay long."

"Father expects me to keep you safe and get you home."

"Never mind about that. I'll find someone to see me safely home."

"You always do the same thing, and you're never bothered about me."

"Don't be silly. There'll be girls here, too. You might like a few of them."

After Peter checked her wrap, she said, "Right then, you have a dance or two with me while I have a look around. Then when I give the nod you just leave and find someone else to dance with."

"I know. I know. What about getting home?"

"Just be late enough that I get there first. Father won't care if it's you out late."

"How late do I have to be?"

"Late."

"And you?"

"Don't you worry about me. I'll be quite all right."

At the entrance they paid separately and entered the dance area.

"I know what's coming next," Peter smirked. "I see it in your eyes. You're a predator, you know."

"Stop talking. I need to concentrate before I decide which one I want."

Peter sighed but obediently stopped talking while Edith examined the men. She knew how to use her eyes to attract the ones she wanted to meet, but she enjoyed looking over her choices before settling on one.

"Now just have a dance or two with me while I have a look around. It won't take long, so don't complain."

They danced, looking like any other couple, with the men in uniform and young women in satin or chiffon. The low light of the room concealed the wear on the dresses. Every young woman wanted new dresses, but had to be cautious about the use of ration coupons. Hems were mended and precious sequins sewn back on, even if they were cracked.

"Right then," she said to Peter. "Usual routine."

"I know. I know. It isn't like we've never been through it before!"

They danced to swing, to "In the Mood" and "The Boogie Woogie Bugle Boy from Company B" while she searched the room, examining the possibilities.

Peter felt Edith stiffen slightly, with a new tension in her body.

"Have you spotted a target?" He couldn't resist teasing, knowing she was attracted to someone.

A blonde man, with eyes the colour of her dress and wearing an RAF uniform, stood at the back of a group. They were all airmen, but he was taller and slimmer than any other. The others were smiling and chatting and looking at girls, but he stood back, silent and serious.

"Shut up and do as I say. Swing me around a bit and keep swinging me in that direction. Land me right in front of that one when the music stops."

"How am I supposed to know which one? Your instructions are rather vague you know."

"Stop talking. That one. Right there."

"Ah, I see." Peter followed the direction of her eyes. "RAF? On his own?"

"I'm going to make that one smile," she told Peter.

"What?"

"Just keep dancing. Now swing me around a bit."

"Not again?"

"Just do as I say. . . . Right then . . . now!"

Peter continued to lead Edith toward the tall man who was standing near the far wall. He needed no further instructions, as her gestures were orders and he understood them. They moved closer to the wall when the music was ending. The demand for the final flourish was to swirl Edith and have her land right in front of the tall man. Peter knew the routine and understood when he would be free to leave.

She spun her body and swirled her dress and smiled directly at the tall man. He blushed and took a step back. His companions began to smile at Edith, but they understood. They stepped aside from the man she so clearly wanted, making it impossible for him to hide from her smile and encouraged him to react to her.

"Come on, then," one insisted. "It's you she wants."

"Why stand there?" another asked while giving the tall man a push forward.

The push made him step toward Edith, and one step was all that was necessary. There was a pause, and then a note from a single saxophone. A moment later, she and Harald were dancing to "Moonlight Serenade."

Harald had never been to a city other than Toronto, and most of his time there had been spent in the air or in barracks. When he arrived in England, he was assigned to barracks again.

He had always been shy about approaching girls. He preferred to stay at the back of a room, on his own. He was used to being on his own when flying. The Spitfire was a small plane and carried only one man. It was fast and versatile, and he was proud of it. It was lighter than the Hurricane, which could take a few hits; a Spitfire would go down on the first.

The Lancaster crews stayed together at the dances, as they did when in the air. They were the rowdy ones, always laughing and drinking in their groups of seven. If the plane went down, all seven of them would go down together, possibly on the way to a target in Germany, possibly while bombing Berlin, possibly on the way back. Wherever they might be, they would be together, and that was the way they were at the dances and in the pubs.

"They keep each other company," said Edith, referring to the Lancaster crews. "You're all alone."

"It isn't completely lonely," Harald told her. "You can see into the other cockpits. . . . You can look into the face of the man you are trying to kill while he is looking at yours while trying to kill you . . ."

"How horrible."

"No. You always understand the other man. . . . It would be easier to hate him, but sometimes it feels as though you are best mates."

"That must be horrible. Oh, I love this piece. Do you know it?"

"'In the Mood'? Everyone knows it."

When they danced, her skirt swirled out and the lights continued to make the sequins on the chiffon sparkle.

"You're not English," she said when the music stopped.

"Norwegian."

"From Oslo?" She tilted her head, inviting conversation.

"A village north of Oslo." He was clearly a man of few words.

"Is it cold?"

"Sometimes, but it is always beautiful."

She chose to let him continue dancing through the next few bars of music before replying.

"I'd love to see Norway."

"Perhaps you will some day."

***

Peter watched and saw that his sister had no further need of him. He had done everything Edith had told him to do, so it was his turn to examine potential dance partners. His sister had been right when she said he might like a few. Even then, when clothing rations made it hard, they were all dressed for dancing. He had a choice of any kind of girl but liked to stay back and look at them first. When he was dancing with Edith, she insisted that he do whatever she wanted, but as soon as she started dancing with someone else, he was free to enjoy the view of pretty faces and nice legs.

He asked a pretty girl to dance, and then danced with one girl after another, always sneaking glances at Edith, remembering that Father saw him as her protector. One of his partners noticed.

"That's not nice! You're dancing with me but you keep looking at her!"

"Who?" He had no idea why his dance partner was upset.

"That one in blue. The one showing off her legs."

"She's my sister."

"Not likely! You can jolly well find someone else to dance with!" She pushed him away and left him standing alone on the dance floor. Other dancers, seeing his red cheeks, must have assumed he had said something improper.

***

Edith said little while dancing with Harald, letting him lead her across the floor, while her skirts swirled out, the sequins sparkling. They danced until the band said goodnight.

Edith gave Peter a signal with her eyes and then turned to Harald.

"Oh, dear, I don't see my brother. He was supposed to get me home safely."

"It would be my pleasure to see you home if you will allow me."

"Oh, *would* you? Oh, thank you so much!"

They collected Edith's wrap and walked toward the Thames. They walked along the Embankment, the water sparkling with the reflections of the street lamps. A moment later, the river turned black when an air raid siren began and the streetlights went dark.

"We need a shelter," Harald said.

"The tube, over there."

They joined everyone else on the pavement, running toward the station. Some people screamed when they heard the explosion of a nearby bomb. They moved down the stairs into the darkest part of the station and then descended to the platform. They sat on the concrete, Edith oblivious to the damage to her dress, and Harald put his arm around her. Some people chatted with others, but most were silent, listening for clues of what was happening on the surface.

***

Edith did not notice Peter nearby. He saw her with the same RAF pilot she had danced with, and decided not to motion to her. Instead, he greeted a pretty girl.

"Hullo, are you all right?"

"Yes, frightened, though." She seemed willing to accept him as a protector.

"We all are. Are you alone?" He smiled in the way he would if offering to get her a drink.

"Yes."

"I'll stay with you if you like." He leaned toward her, smiling.

"Are you on your own?"

"Yes, all by myself. I've just come from a dance."

"You went alone?"

"Yes, why not?" He shrugged.

***

Edith knew before they had finished their first dance that she would see Harald again, and he knew the same thing. The uniform he wore at the dance was his standard clothing and the only clothing he wore in public. Edith's swirling blue dress was returned to her wardrobe while she went about her daily life in uniform.

They met as a military couple, like so many others. Their usual meeting place was St. James' Park, in the same area where Pat enjoyed chasing pigeons. Those were calm times, and even though they were constantly aware of the background of war, they could stroll, hand in hand, and enjoy each moment of peace.

During the calm times, the people who hurried through tube stations in the evening usually had the same reasons as the people who hurry through them now, but in those days, they often had another reason.

"Oh, bloody hell!" Edith said when a siren sounded.

"Victoria's the closest," Harald answered.

"Right then—into the tube."

The tube was not always a safe place. One station, with shallow tunnels, collapsed during a bomb raid and provided no shelter to those who sought it. Most stations had tunnels deep enough to provide safety for the night, either on a regular basis or when caught out for an evening. Many people kept blankets and clothing in specific places and set up homes away from home on the platforms. Children's cots could be slung, hammock style, between the rails. It was important to ignore the smells of soot and trains and unwashed blankets, and lack of toilet facilities.

The bombing of the Guards' Chapel was one bombing among many. The prime minister was known to stand on rooftops during air raids, watching the explosions, while he was supposed to be in the underground Cabinet War Rooms. After the bombing of the chapel, as after other bombings, a plant grew in the patches of earth beneath debris, sending shoots and leaves and flowers up through the rubble. The plant, *Saxifraga x urbium*, was known as London Pride. Shoots of the plant, growing up through rubble in a damaged railway station, inspired Noel Coward. His song "London Pride" became a hit, allowing people to remember their own courage and resilience.

BAVARIA
December 1941

Marta tried to keep the traditions of a German Christmas. She decorated the windows with angels and stars cut out of old newspapers. The paper could be used for kindling in January so there was no waste. She had flour, and Frau Geller—who was in favour, with two sons in the SS—had given her some dried fruit. She was grateful to Frau Geller but resented having nothing to give in return. Her tears fell into the dough as she was mixing it. The stollen would not be as it should, but it would be a reminder of things as she had known them.

Konrad, on the other hand, did nothing to celebrate the season. He failed to follow even his own traditions. Marta's shame at her lack of the expected luxuries was compounded by shame at her husband's failure to support their community in even the most basic way.

"You did not make toys for the village this year. Have you no pride?"

"I am tired when I get home."

"Is that your excuse?"

"I walk miles every day to muck a barn."

"Yes, and you know the reason." She hammered rather than kneaded the dough.

"I go because we need to eat."

"That and because you are a fool. You have given up everything."

"I know, and Hannes Kaufmann heckles me."

"Why shouldn't he? You could have stayed in that job, and now he has it."

Konrad looked at the floor and said nothing in reply.

"Being a policeman was a position with respect. Now, you have the respect of no one."

"Not even you?" He looked at her, hoping for a sign of recognition of their marriage as it had been.

"Not even yourself I hope!"

"Marta, I could never be that kind of policeman."

"One kind is the same as another. They make people obey the laws."

Konrad remained silent, hoping she would stop. She softened her attack on the dough and smiled. "Frau Geller told me the Fuehrer is coming to this area to visit soldiers. We should go to see him."

"Nein, Leibchen, not for me."

"Why not? We must show our loyalty."

She was determined to see the great leader, if only from a distance, whether or not her husband would. She could go with Frau Geller, who was widowed. That would make the absence of a husband less conspicuous.

LONDON
1942

Nearly everyone had a uniform. It wasn't just the military. The postmen, the policemen, the fire fighters, and others wore distinctive clothing.

Terry Jones, who lived with his mum and dad just a few houses down the road from the Edwards family, wanted a uniform, too. When he turned fourteen, he finished his mandatory schooling and decided to go out to work. Everyone else was involved in the war effort in some way. His dad led scrap drives and put up posters at the pub, and his mum spent most of her time away from home making bandages. Everyone else was serving the King. Nearly everyone had a uniform and he wanted one, too.

When he saw a telegram boy, in his neat pillbox hat, he knew he could have a uniform despite being too young to enlist. The uniform was navy blue with red piping trim and a red button on the hat. It looked quite smart and set off a young man's figure. Having a job as a telegram boy meant he could have a bicycle without facing the risk that it might be taken away on a scrap metal drive.

Mr. and Mrs. Jones saved ration coupons and had real tea, rather than tea made from leaves, and were enjoying a pot of it in their front room when Terry came in, wearing his natty uniform.

"What's this?" asked Mrs. Jones.

"I'm serving the King, Mum. I'm in uniform."

"Don't ever let me see you in any other uniform."

"Lad, I agree with your mum." Mr. Jones put his tea down. "Let's hope this war ends before you're told to have any job other than the one you have."

"I'm serving the King however I'm needed, Dad."

"Yes, and the job you have is important. Do it well, and go on with it as long as you can."

His dad was calmer than his mum, who had been fidgeting from the time he walked in, when she saw the unform.

Terry took pride in his bike. He washed it and polished the metal every day, whether or not he was on duty, just as he kept his uniform neat and clean and kept the little button on the pillbox hat secure. Terry knew that, just as much as any older boy in uniform, he was serving the King, and going about the King's business. Everyone on the road knew Terry and he knew them. He did not understand why people looked at him in a different way when he went out in his uniform.

On his first day, Terry had three telegrams to deliver. The first was to the Reid's house. He knew Mrs. Reid's father had been ill, so he wasn't surprised at her reaction.

"Oh, I must catch the next train. Yes, Terry, I do wish to send a reply."

The next telegram was to Miss Baker's house.

"Oh, now isn't that lovely! Mary remembered my birthday. No need for a reply, lad; I'll write a note."

Terry didn't know the people at the third house. When the lady who opened the door saw him, she stepped back and screamed.

Terry could not alternate his calls. He quickly learned that his smart uniform, even with its red piping trim, was no armour against the emotions of the people receiving the telegrams. Nor did he have the option of thinking, "Maybe next year" or "This one will be all right anyway." For the people receiving the telegrams there could be no "next year" and no way to make it "all right." Terry, at the age of fourteen, realized that being in a smart-looking uniform was not as glamourous as he had imagined.

People still sent good telegrams, like "Happy Birthday stop Love Jim," "Congratulations stop Love Paul," "Job well done stop Love

Mary," but most were sent on behalf of His Majesty and contained the words "regret to inform you." When people saw Terry riding his bicycle, they would stop whatever they were doing and watch to see which house he approached, hoping it would not be their own. When he went to another door, the feeling of relief that it was not their own door was followed by compassionate pain at the knowledge of what had had happened to their neighbours.

***

Everyone in London understood the reality of the bombings, but they continued to enjoy life as much as they could. Margie Denning understood the danger but always felt proud to be on Harry's arm when they went out together. He cut a handsome figure in his uniform and she liked to chat about her evenings with him when she was in the Rose and Crown.

"Harry took me to the cinema last night," she said to the group at the dart board. "That *Mrs. Miniver* is a jolly good film. Shows this country as we are!"

The film *Mrs. Miniver* showed them Hollywood's idealized version of their way of life: continuing to live life with neighbours and go about their daily business while knowing that bombs could fall. It was an effective way for Hollywood to make them feel proud to be British.

The cinema gave people time away from war, but reality continued. Air raid sirens usually gave them enough time to get to the shelters. Everyone with a house had an Anderson shelter in the back garden, and there were designated shelters for people who were away from home.

The parish hall of St. Peter's Church was a designated shelter. The church was at the end of the street Edith lived on. Edith and her stepmother, Anne, volunteered there, baking and making tea and sandwiches while people were taking shelter, and cutting cloth into bandages at other times. Those times were social, as well as serious. The women cutting cloth could laugh with each other about things their children had done, and share the latest gossip. Edith found it a way to stay in touch with the neighbours, as well as her family. Cutting cloth became a way to enjoy a day out, while serving King and country. Not every day was enjoyable.

One day while they were cutting cloth for bandages, the siren began to wail. Everyone in the parish hall looked up, not noticing the direction of anyone else's eyes but as a reflex, staring at the ceiling as if they could see through it to find the trajectory of a plane. The wail of the siren and the engines of the bombers competed, as though one being louder than the other would give victory. The sounds on the outside were in contrast to the silence within, where no one spoke or even breathed loudly. They were holding their collective breath when the silence was ended by the crash of the roof, falling down onto their tables and opening the view of the sky above.

Everyone on the street knew the need for quick action. People in houses or shops mobilized, even though it meant leaving their own shelters. Edith was rescued quickly, but Anne was in the rubble. Edith waited and waited while some survivors, and many bodies, were pulled out, but there was no sign of Anne.

Edith understood that on the death of Anne, she would have to become the mother figure for Pat and her little brothers. Edith was young, but she had to accept the end of her evenings of dancing.

Rain began to fall while Edith waited, watching the rescue crews sort through the rubble of the bombed building. Rain was welcome, wetting the dust and cooling the searchers. A woman sat bedside Edith, preventing her from running to the bomb site.

"You've been hurt, dear. All you can do right now is sit . . . sit and wait."

The woman held her hand while the two of them watched men remove chunks of plaster and wood and brick. They worked in a line, handing pieces of the parish hall from one to another. They understood the need for speed in rescuing survivors; they also understood the need to work slowly and methodically to avoid causing weight to fall and crush anyone who might otherwise live. Their clothing was torn and their faces muddy with the wet dust as they removed piece after piece of the building.

"Somebody 'ere!" a man shouted.

At first there was a sense of excitement and an urgency to move quickly. The excitement ended when the man who had shouted carried out the limp body of a small boy. A man was also pulled from the rubble, still alive but unconscious, with blood flowing from his head.

"All righty, then! If he's bleedin', he's alive."

There were other people pulled out: some alive, some dead, some in pieces. The dead were a light grey, the colour of ghosts. The living ones were almost the same colour.

"Somebody 'ere," another man shouted. "Right then, let's dig."

"What is it?"

"I see a foot, with a woman's shoe."

"Right then, let's get the rest of 'er."

Edith recognized Anne's shoe and saw that blood was flowing from the leg. Flowing blood. Life. She moved forward, wanting to get up and go to Anne, but was restrained by a woman who had miraculously produced a cup of tea.

"No, Dear." The woman held her gently. "You've been injured. Let them do their work."

"My stepmum's in there. I have to get her."

"No, dear." The woman held her more firmly. "The only way you can help her is by letting the men do their work."

"I have to see . . ." She started to sit up.

"No." The woman held her back. "Stay here and take a few sips of this."

Edith wanted to refuse the tea, but the warmth of it was comforting.

"That's it. Take it all, Dear."

The men, covered with dust, making them the same colour as ashes, pulled pieces of plaster and wood out quickly in some places to reach the victims, and slowly in others, to prevent the remnants of the walls from collapsing. When they uncovered Anne's face, it was the same grey as the faces of the dead and the faces of the dust-covered rescuers. The only thing indicating life was the blood flowing along her leg.

"Got 'er!" one man said. "We'll need two more blokes to lift 'er out. She's right limp."

The woman with the tea smiled at Edith. "There you are, Dear. She's out. She'll need a right bit of attention, but she's out."

Anne needed hospital care and then the use of a cane for the next few months, so Edith stayed with her as often as she could. They wanted their old routines and followed them as much as they could.

They continued to have tea in the afternoon. With their tea, they pretended to have biscuits and jam, but there was no jam, nor were there any biscuits. Not long after, they took their tea without milk because there was no milk. Then they took their tea without lemon because there were no lemons. Finally, they took their tea without tea because there was no tea.

They still used the teapot, warming it properly, every afternoon, but the leaves they used were from rose bushes or patches of mint or anything else that might be palatable. Linden tree blossoms were acceptable, especially when blended with beech buds. The problem was finding the linden and beech trees.

BAVARIA
1942

Konrad Meier wondered about the Reiber family. Johannes Dortmund had been killed in France, but Heinrich Reiber occasionally returned to the village on leave. His older brother, Friedrich, had not been chosen to serve the Reich and continued to work on the farm. Heinrich did not drink beer with his brother when he was home on leave, or spend time with him in public.

When he was a policeman, Konrad never had trouble from Friedrich, but the Brownshirts sometimes stopped Friedrich in the streets and kicked him. Every kick knocked him to the ground because of his bad leg. He had been injured when he was a child, and the leg never healed properly. A crutch helped, but he was set aside as an invalid. Friedrich stayed to himself and helped his mother at home.

"That one is strange," Marta declared. "He has never had a girl."

"It's a man's choice not to," Konrad said.

"No. A man chooses to be with a woman . . . always. If not, there is something wrong."

"It has nothing to do with us."

"He should be serving the Fatherland."

"He has had a bad leg since he was a child."

"His limp is not bad, and he does not have to be a soldier."

"What then?"

"There are other things he could do, but he does nothing. I will speak to Hannes Kaufmann about him."

"Just to make trouble? Hannes Kaufmann is a bully. I arrested him many times."

When he went to the market the next day, Konrad noticed Marta chatting with Frau Kaufmann and glancing toward Frau Reiber. Hannes Kaufmann joined them and listened while Marta gestured toward Frau Reiber. The three of them spoke quietly, nodding in obvious agreement with each other.

Later in the afternoon, while Konrad was enjoying a beer on his porch, Friedrich Reiber approached and nodded a greeting.

"A lovely day, Herr Meier." He paused to chat, smiling, while leaning on his cane.

"So it his. How is your mother?"

"Still worried about my brother. She misses him and prays for his safe return."

"As do we all." Konrad gestured to the other chair. "Will you sit with me? I have not seen you lately."

"You are very kind, but I must go. My mother worries about me, too."

"Tell your mother to let you stop and sit with me some day soon." Konrad held out his hand and then hesitated before continuing. "Tell me, Friedrich, have you been well?"

"As well as can be, Herr Meier. My mother worries needlessly." He shook his head. "She behaves as though I should be in the house all day."

Konrad noticed Hannes Kaufmann walking toward them, holding something in his hand.

"Perhaps she is right. Sometimes, it is good to go unnoticed."

"This is yours." Hannes Kaufmann threw a pink triangle at Friedrich. "Sew it on and see me at seven o'clock."

Human beings were labelled according to assigned categories. Yellow stars for Jews, pink triangles for homosexual men, red triangles for communists and other political prisoners, green triangles for common criminals, and black triangles for Gypsies and those "asocial." The black triangles would also be on lesbians, draft dodgers, the "work shy," the homeless, prostitutes, the mentally ill, pacifists, aristocrats, or any others considered undesirable.

That was the last time Konrad saw Friedrich Reiber.

ENGLAND
1942

"I have some leave next week," Harald told Edith.

"So do I! Have you been to Brighton?"

Like all military couples, they planned every moment of their leave. While at Brighton or Eastbourne or any other seaside town, they could buy cockles and winkles from women on the beach or fish and chips wrapped in newspaper showing the headlines of the previous day through blotches of grease.

"It's lovely to have some things not rationed," Edith said, biting into a piece of hot fish.

There were fish in the sea and potatoes in the earth, so there was no need to ration them. Couples walked along the promenade, enjoying the comforting seaside blend of salt mist, fish and the malt vinegar on their fingers. The planes and boats they watched were not pleasure craft, and the pier was blocked by barbed wire.

A flight of Lancasters flew over, heading out toward the Channel in straight lines toward France.

"Where do you think they're off too?" Edith asked.

"I don't know. Somewhere in Germany. Maybe Berlin." He watched the sky as intently as she did.

"It always bothers me to see them flying out."

"I know. We should stay and wait . . . to watch a few flying home." He put his arm around her, wanting to give comfort.

"They always fly in such straight lines." She spoke quietly, leaning against him while watching the planes.

"No reason to do anything else. . . . When you are going on a mission, you just want to get it done. . . . When you are coming back . . . well, that's obvious . . . you want to be back as soon as you can."

"The others fly in straight lines, too."

"Of course. They feel the same way. We want to kill them, and they want to kill us, but we all feel the same way." There was sadness in his voice. "Sometimes you shoot at someone and want to buy him a beer."

Flying over France and the Low Countries, Harald knew in theory where the borders were, but there were places where they were not clearly defined. There were places where the borders were not marked by rivers or roads or even fences. The landscape was the same across the area, with each country having its own character on the ground, its own national identity, and yet sharing the same soil and the same landscape.

***

Pat was upset that her older sister would live in barracks.

"That's as it has to be, darling. All of us military girls have to live in barracks, but you can visit me and I'll visit you as much as I can."

Edith was stationed in London, so the visits were frequent. For Pat, a trip to Wellington Barracks also meant stopping outside Buckingham Palace and hoping for a glimpse of the King and Queen. A visit there would also include walks in the park and possibly a visit to another special place.

"I'm taking you to Lyons," Edith would say.

The first time Pat heard that she thought it meant a trip to the zoo to see lions and tigers. Edith's plan was much more glamourous. The only lions they would see were the stone ones around the statue of Lord Nelson. Lyons Tea Room was on the corner of The Strand, across from Trafalgar Square. Edith checked Pat's face and hair and dusted off any bits she might have on her dress. Pat automatically sat properly in Lyons. There were white table cloths and uniformed waitresses. They had real tea, with milk or lemon, and real biscuits and scones with strawberry jam and clotted cream.

"How do they get these things?" Pat was in awe of the things on the table, unable to remember when she had seen such treats before.

"Restaurants aren't rationed, darling."

"Why not?" The child was genuinely curious.

"I'm not sure."

"Why is everyone else rationed?"

"To make sure we don't run out of food." Edith tried to smile.

"I don't understand."

"What? What don't you understand?"

"If restaurants aren't rationed, then can't rich people eat all they want just by going to restaurants?"

"Aren't you the clever girl!" She nodded, in appreciation of her sister's childhood wisdom. "People a lot older than you have been asking the same question."

Older people had noticed the same unfairness as Pat. The rules were changed, limiting the number of courses and the combinations of food that could be served at restaurants. Fortunately for Pat and Edith, the new rules did not change things at Lyons Tea Room.

***

Edith visited the family as often as she could. Their London house was still the place where she kept her dresses and dancing shoes.

Sirens could scream at any time of day or night. The blackout curtains were always up, and the gas masks were always kept secure on pegs by the door. Anne had stocked the Anderson shelter with tinned food and blankets. Father had stocked it with his favourite liquid refreshments.

Everyone knew what to do when they heard the first siren. It was real, and they knew the bombs were real, too.

"Right then, off to the garden," Anne and Edith and Father said it, almost in unison, before gathering Pat and Jimmy and taking them to the shelter.

No one measured time while listening to the sirens and the planes and the explosions. No one spoke. It was as though silence had to be observed as carefully as the blackout. There was no logical possibility that whispers in the Anderson shelter could be heard by the pilots dropping bombs, but logic did not seem helpful. Logic did not apply.

After a while, Pat began to cough. Time after time, in the damp earth and darkness, she would cough and the cough kept getting worse. Then her breathing changed and she gasped for each breath.

"She needs a doctor," Edith said.

"Yes, I've taken her," Anne explained. "It's asthma. Being in here doesn't help."

When the raid ended, they would leave the shelter, wet and dirty despite Anne's best efforts to keep it homey, and look out at their street to see what, if anything, was left of it. So far, they were lucky that time: all the houses on their street were as they had been each day before, but the soot smell from the next street reminded them of their vulnerability.

The soot smell became pervasive, as the raids went on. The family lived with the smell of soot and high explosives on the street, and in the garden; it seeped into the house, and was only slightly less inside the house than in the shelter. It grew stronger after each raid, and dissipated only slightly before the next one. One such raid began as Edith was just about to go dancing.

"Bedtime?" Edith had asked Pat after letting the child watch her prepare for the dance. "You've seen me do my face and you chose my dress, and now, I'm all ready to go. Hug and kiss and then off you go."

Pat was reaching for the hug when a siren began.

"Oh, bloody hell! Come on, then, into the Anderson with you. Where are the others?"

By the time Edith had taken Pat downstairs, the others were already there, in the back hall, holding gas masks and the blankets that were always kept on a bench beside the back door.

"Right then, I suppose I'll have to put out my pipe," Father admitted.

"Yes, you will." Anne was direct. "Out we go, then."

The others started through the door, toward the shelter, but Edith paused and Anne waited for her to move.

"Edie, what are you waiting for?"

"I'm not going in there."

"What?"

"Here, you go in. Take care of the children. I'm ready to go dancing, and that's what I'll do."

"Darling, you could get killed."

"I could get killed anyway."

Father and the children were already in the shelter. Anne knew there would be no point in trying to change Edith's mind, but she still hesitated.

"Look here—you go into that shelter. They need you. I've got my gas mask, and I'm going out dancing."

"Is it really wise to go out?"

"No, it isn't wise, but I'm still going."

"Edie, we don't want anything bad happening to you. You'll be safe in the shelter, and there'll be lots of other times to go dancing."

"I know." Edith looked directly at Anne. "But there's a reason I have to go dancing."

"Now, what on earth might that be?"

"I'm standing up to Hitler." She said it calmly, and the statement was matter of fact, but Anne didn't see how dancing could win the war.

"Whatever do you mean by that?"

"Don't you see? We're all being frightened by old Adolf and weakened by our own fear. Yes, I might get hurt or even killed, but it would be on my terms, not old Adolf's." She spoke with vehemence. "He might be able to end my life, but he'll bloody well not run it. If I want to go dancing, I'll go dancing."

Anne was quiet for a moment before answering. "Right you are. Here then, give me a kiss and don't get caught by the warden!"

"I'll be fine; the warden's Mr. Carson tonight, and he likes me."

Mr. Carson examined every house and every shop while doing his rounds in the darkness. It might have been his imagination, but it seemed that his own footsteps were louder than the siren and would alert the pilots flying over London to his own presence, and to that of the houses and shops in his neighbourhood. It wasn't an important area by military measures, as there were no ships or planes, no army barracks, no government buildings, and nothing of any more importance than ordinary people trying to survive. He knew all that in his mind, but not in his heart. The people in the dark houses were his neighbours, and he had assumed the responsibility of protecting them from the dangers of glowing cigarettes and gaping blackout curtains. Those thoughts dominated his mind, but he craved the comfort of a cigarette.

Most people, even the young boys, understood the dangers and cooperated. Even so, he wasn't surprised to see a young woman coming around a corner, and he knew who it was.

"Edie! Where do you think you're off to!" he exclaimed rather than asked.

"It's all right, Mr. Carson." She gave him her most flirtatious smile.

"No, lass, it's not all right. There's an air raid on. Get yourself along into a shelter! I'll not have you staying out here!"

"I can't." She started to use tears rather than smiles. "I hate it in there."

"Aye, lass." He softened. "We all do."

Edith saw that Mr. Carson's expression was not the same jolly face she knew from the pub. She realized they were the only people sharing the darkness of the street. He had put his own life at risk to protect his neighbours and he looked a tired man, smaller and weaker than when singing at the Rose and Crown.

"All right, Mr. Carson; I'll be at the bus stop in two minutes."

"And what's the point of that, lass? There'll be no buses running before the all clear. Get off with you now, into a shelter, and be a good girl."

He was right about the lack of buses, so she went to Mr. Carson's own house and surprised his wife by asking admission to their Anderson shelter.

LONDON
1943

Lyons was always welcoming and adding a bit of "posh" to the lives of working class people. Very few could afford to dine at Rules, but Lyons was for everyone, and treated everyone as "special". A toff could pop in, as well as a dustman.

The nippies—waitresses with neat black dresses, trimmed with crisp white collars and cuffs and wearing starched white aprons—were chosen more for pleasant personalities than for looks, which meant everyone in Lyons always felt special, and the nippies were always kind to Pat. Pat knew that a visit to Lyons meant scones with jam and clotted cream, and real tea.

Edith was always in uniform when they went to Lyons, but Pat didn't associate that with clothing rations or understand that Edith didn't want to spoil the few nice dresses she had left. All the other women in Edith's barracks wore their uniforms when they went out, so it didn't seem strange.

It did seem strange, or at least unusual, to see how long Edith took to do her makeup one afternoon when Pat visited. She took as much care, and as much time, as she had when they were in the house and Edith was getting ready to drag Peter to a dance.

"I thought we were going to Lyons." Pat was puzzled.

"We are." Edith gave no hint of any reason for her special care with makeup.

"Why are you doing your face like that?"

"Never you mind." The words were sharp, but Edith was holding back a smile.

It was the same response Edith had given Pat many times before, and she knew there was no point in asking other questions. Edith finished her lipstick and handed Pat her jacket.

"Right then. Come along. Let's not dawdle."

Edith said nothing while they left the barracks, walked across the park, passed Trafalgar Square, onto the Strand, and into Lyons Corner House.

"Good afternoon, miss," the hostess greeted Edith. "And to you, young miss." She smiled at Pat and gestured toward a table.

"Oh, not there." Edith stopped her and smiled at a man in RAF uniform who had stood up at a table on the other side of the room. Pat had never seen him before, but she understood.

"Oh, Edie, he's handsome!"

"Yes, and nice, too. Come on, and I'll introduce you."

The man held out his hand toward Edith, and they touched the tips of their fingers.

"This is my sister, Pat. Darling, this is Harald."

Pat noticed that instead of looking at her, as people usually do when being introduced, he looked at Edith and she looked at him. Then he turned to Pat and gave her a grownup's handshake. Pat felt like a fine lady when he held her chair for her before doing the same for Edith.

Tea at Lyons involved a careful ceremony: the waitress in her black uniform and white apron brought each item to the table in a set order and placed it in a set place. Pat sat up straight, remaining silent and waiting for Edith's signal that she could begin.

"Here, try one of these little round ones. They're pretty, aren't they?" Edith smiled and moved the plate toward Pat.

"They taste nice, too." Harald gestured at the prettiest sandwiches.

Edith did most of the talking. Harald was quiet, but he smiled a lot. Pat liked his smile, and it was clear that Edith liked it, too. When he did speak, his voice was soft and he spoke slowly, with an accent Pat didn't recognize. She knew she shouldn't ask him what it was, but she could ask Edith later.

"Do you like tea, Pat?" he asked.

"Yes, I do. This is my favourite tea room."

She was embarrassed when Edith smiled and said, "I thought it was the only tea room you know." When the child's smile disappeared, Edith corrected her error with, "Let's take you to a few others; would you like that?"

Pat's smile returned, and she nodded.

Harald made another suggestion. "Do you like birds, Pat? Do you like to feed them?" He leaned toward her, as though no one else should hear.

"Yes."

"So do I. Would you like to feed birds after we've had our tea?"

"Oh, yes!" When she blurted it out, the people at the next table turned to look at her.

Harald excused himself from the table, went to the front of the room, and spoke briefly to the hostess, gesturing back toward the little girl. Pat noticed the hostess smile and nod. When they left, she gave him a bag with scraps of bread crust and a small bag of crumbs, taking care to avoid letting anyone else notice.

"Pigeons or ducks?" he asked.

"But they're all pigeons in Trafalgar Square."

"Yes, but we could walk to the park to see ducks, and there are pigeons there, too. Which would you like?"

"Oh, the park!"

A few minutes later, they were in St. James' Park, and Pat was feeding pigeons, despite the ban on wasting crumbs during rationing.

"I have to get back tonight," Harald mentioned to Edith while Pat chased the birds. "Something over the Channel. I won't have much leave in the next little while. They're talking about special assignments."

"I don't know what to say about that." She leaned toward him. "It sounds dangerous."

He pulled her toward him and kissed her forehead. "It's always dangerous, but we've known that all along."

She pushed him back. "Yes, but that doesn't mean I have to like it." She paused and softened her voice. "Oh, I'm sorry. I know you have to go, and I'm ever so proud of you." She leaned against him again, welcoming another hug.

The next evening, Harald was one of many pilots, in one of many planes, ready for an assignment. They flew up, over the fields of Sussex, over Beachy Head, just off Eastbourne, and out over the Channel and the coast of France. After dusk, Harald could see the lights of Eastbourne and the reflections on the water. The glow of moonlight against the white chalk cliff at Beachy Head would guide them home.

The town of Eastbourne was created as a seaside holiday resort, from the pier to the Grand Hotel, near the slope going up to the top of Beachy Head, a cliff that dominated the area. The Grand was set back from the sea front, slightly elevated, allowing the guests to look down on beachgoers. The wealthy guests would bring their own maids and valets, who would dress them for afternoon tea and dinner each day. There was always music. The BBC broadcast Palm Court music from the Grand, even though there was no palm court. Guests and staff at the Grand understood the significance whenever the orchestra played a piece by Debussy, who used his stay at the Grand to compose.

All those things were before the War. The size of the hotel made it an obvious place for a military headquarters, so the silk dresses and fine suits gave way to uniforms. Soldiers took comfort, like the locals, in strolling along the seaside promenade, as though they were tourists.

BAVARIA
1943

"They've bombed the church!" Marta screamed while running into the house.

Konrad remained still, sipping beer and working on a puzzle on the only table left after burning furniture for fuel.

"Many things have been bombed," Konrad said quietly.

"Everything . . . everything is destroyed. . . . We cannot see our baptism papers or our wedding papers." She began to cry.

"Not everything has been destroyed. We have our lives . . . that's something."

"All the old papers burned. . . . Everything about this village . . . about everyone who has ever lived here!"

"There were other people here, too. . . . People who did not go to the church."

"Stop thinking about those Jews! They are gone. We are free of them!" Her crying gave way to screaming.

"What happened to Friedrich Reiber?" Konrad was hesitant, but he had to ask. "I know you had something to do with it."

"What of it? We are free of his kind, too. The Fuehrer will make us a clean people."

Konrad left without speaking and went to his garden. Marta remained in the kitchen and took risen dough from the cupboard. Punching down the dough was the only reaction she could think of.

Beverley Dowling

"Silly man," she said aloud. "Worrying about Jews and undesirables! He should worry about our fine soldiers! . . . He should be in uniform himself. . . . He is not too old. . . . He could be proud in a fine uniform."

She shaped the dough and slapped it onto a baking stone. She looked outside and saw Konrad, her husband, digging in the garden.

"The fool! He thinks planting potatoes will save us from his stupidity."

LONDON
1943

When Pat told her parents about Harald, they became anxious to meet him. Edith arranged to make it look casual, as though they were simply dropping in one afternoon, even though the tube and buses took over an hour. They had travelled by tube from Victoria Station to Euston, where they changed to the Northern line to Archway, where they changed to a northbound bus, which had a stop within walking distance of the house. Edith and Harald were both in uniform, as usual. Father was happy to sit in his usual chair, while Anne poured tea and chatted.

"Edie tells us you're from Norway," Anne smiled at Harald, "We're very glad to have you with us. Now, do you take one teaspoon or two?"

"Oh, no, please do not use your sugar this way!" He held his hand over his tea.

"Nonsense. It's our pleasure."

"Oh, but please, just a very little."

"As I said, it's our pleasure," Anne said while Father worried about whether there would be enough sugar left for him.

"You are very kind."

"We're all on the same side. I'd like to think that if one of our boys got washed up on a Norwegian shore, some nice lady would give him sugar for his tea."

He blushed slightly when she added more sugar to his tea.

"Not if he's a Navy man." Father couldn't resist commenting. "A tot of rum would be more his cup of tea."

"When were you last in the garden?" Anne glared. "How are your marrows?"

"My marrows are as they are, and I'm not going out to them again."

Edith and Harald glanced at each other, suppressing smiles.

"So, young man," Father spoke, "how long will you be on leave?"

"It was supposed to be for another four days, but they've called me in for tomorrow."

"Bloody unfair that. Can't make plans." Father was sympathetic to Harald. He knew the family made fun of his boasting about his service in the last war, but his experience was real and he understood the disappointment of cancelled leaves.

Despite his bluster, Father understood the reality of Harald's life, and Harald recognized that understanding in Father. He also noticed the little dog, which stayed beside Father's chair. No one else seemed to notice the dog's knowledge of their own habits. It was clear to Harald that the dog knew exactly when Father would drop a piece of bread and make it look like an accident.

RAF BARRACKS
1943

Harald was back in barracks the next day and was asked to attend the group captain's post. The two men could have been brothers, both tall, slim, and blonde; the senior officer only a few years older. Their accents were the biggest difference: one being Nordic and the other English public school.

Harald wondered why he was called to the inner office. He had followed all the rules and got along well with everyone. He knew he was a good pilot and had followed all orders. When he approached the office, the door was open and he could see his group captain, William Denham, with another man in the uniform of an army major.

"Ah, do come in." Group Captain Denham smiled as both men rose. "This is Major Sutton. He has asked to see you, specifically."

"For what reason, sir?"

"Your record, my boy!" Major Sutton was warm in his answer. "You have a great deal to be proud of, and you're up for promotion. We want you to know how proud we are of you."

Harald knew this was strange, so he chose to remain silent.

"You are a brilliant pilot." Major Sutton waited for Harald to respond.

Group Captain Denham broke the silence. ""Do sit down. Cigarette?"

"I don't wish to be rude, sir, but I doubt you brought me here to offer a cigarette. There must be some other reason."

The other man hesitated. "Our intelligence people have asked me to give them a bit of help with certain areas. . . ."

Yes. That single sentence made it clear. Harald knew what the questions would be before the first one was asked.

"How are you at operating a camera?" Major Sutton looked straight at Harald while asking.

"The cameras on the wings work well, sir."

"Er, yes . . . but there could be a few other things, too."

Harald waited, aware that Major Sutton was fidgeting and Group Captain Denham was holding his head toward a stack of papers. "What might they be, sir?" he asked Denham.

"We need pilots who could drop off passengers. That part is fairly easy, as they go in by parachute, but picking up the ones coming back is a bit trickier."

"Touch-and-go landings?"

"Very similar." Major Sutton looked grim. "And lots of photographs."

***

Harald took Edith to Brighton when they both had leave. Neither had used the clothing rations, so they were both in uniform: he in RAF, she in her WAAF uniform, complete with peaked cap and black lace-up shoes. It was chilly, so they hugged and leaned against each other, surrounded by the smells of salt mist and the dampened wool of their uniforms, and the cries of gulls.

The mist wet their faces and hair, but she didn't care about the effect on her curls. She could brush them back into place later. They walked past the barriers closing the pier while a sympathetic sentry looked away. They walked to the very end and looked out toward France, seeing nothing but the magnificence of the waves. In that place, at that moment, there was peace.

"They're giving me a new assignment," he said, "but I can't talk to you about it."

She said nothing but didn't have to ask questions. She understood that some things, many things, could not be discussed. He had talked to her freely about his earlier flights, so the secrecy of the new assignment was intriguing. She wanted to know the details, but asking would be wrong. His passion for his work was one of the things she admired most about him. He would never betray his duty, and she should never ask questions.

The next time Harald flew, he was over occupied France. His superiors had detailed knowledge of the area near the coast. The coast had either high cliffs, which would be almost impossible to climb, or wide beaches, which would provide no cover to an invading army. The flatness could make it possible for the invaders to get off the beach quickly, but the lack of cover meant heightened risk for the individual soldiers.

If an army could get past the coast, which was questionable, it would have to continue its advance. For that to happen, detailed information was necessary. Analysts could not assume that old bridges were still in existence or that new ones had not been built. The conditions of roads and bridges may have deteriorated or been improved. The locations and condition of attack and defence equipment was needed. The condition of railway tracks, providing supply lines, was necessary information.

The planes were equipped with wing cameras, but sometimes more detail was needed. A flyer with a camera had to get as close as he could to the objects being photographed, without being shot down. It was a fine balance. The analysts needed the details for many reasons. They had to plan not only an invasion, but also ways to deliver and extract agents, including delivery and extraction by air.

Despite his underlying awareness of danger, there were moments when Harald was distracted by beauty. War and death were evident everywhere, but the sea and the sky continued to change from shades of blue to shades of blue-grey to soft light contrasted against darkness. He struggled to concentrate on his mission, defying the temptation to soar and spin and fly through the clouds. Being in an airplane was something he had dreamed of as a child, growing up in a place where they were never seen, except in picture books. He knew the dangers, but flying had been a dream and he was living it, living his life, even in the face of his own mortality. The beaches stretched out from the cliffs at the west side, through the market towns and villages and farms. The farm houses and barns might be places of danger or places of welcome. Neither would be evident from the air.

***

Even after that, Edith and Harald occasionally found time to visit the seaside. The boats might be those of the fishermen, going about the serious business of providing food, or military vessels of any size. The planes rarely circled but flew in straight lines, directly to a specific destination. They felt relief when watching the planes fly back toward England but held their breath for a moment every time they watched them fly south from Beachy Head, flying over the Channel toward France.

The entire coast was ready for both defence and attack. Even the land girls, who worked on the coastal farms, had been given guns and taught how to use them. Every night, the people at the southeastern edge of the country would be awoken by air raid sirens and stumble out in darkness to the Anderson shelters to attempt sleep. Some removed those shelters as soon as they could after the war, hoping never to see another reminder of them. Others remain in the gardens even now, as storage sheds for rakes and hoes and potting soil.

The beach along that part of the English Channel, where Edith and Harald enjoyed visiting, was not soft sand but shingle pebbles. It was not a place to walk barefoot, and it was easier to stroll along the promenade or the pier rather than risk walking on the stones.

Edith and Harald both understood the dangers of what he was doing while on duty, even though he never shared the details. It made the times together more important, and more intense. It was more important than ever before to go dancing. Whenever they had an evening together they would find an opportunity to dance. They danced to band music, with or without vocalists, but they knew the words to the tunes.

At the dances, they were always dressed as they had been when they met: he in his RAF uniform and she in her blue dress, with sequins sparkling and flashing while her skirt flared out, even though some of the sequins were cracked, and others had gone missing. They danced to "Sing, Sing, Sing"—*"We will sing, sing, sing . . . and make music with the heavens"*—and the slow, dreamy "Moonlight Serenade"—*". . . the roses are sighing . . .*"—and to "A Nightingale Sang in Berkeley Square" played as a foxtrot.

They danced to the misty music of "Somewhere Over the Rainbow," usually without vocal accompaniment. A vocalist was never needed because everyone knew the words—". . .*where troubles melt like lemon drops, away above the chimney tops* . . ."

LONDON
1943

Anne held Edith's hand while studying the ring.

"Oh, Edie, I wish your dad had given me something like that!"

"Yes, but anything from him would be lovely, wouldn't it?"

To be given a ring at all was unexpected. Neither Edith nor Anne could think of how Harald had been able to get the ring, but there it was—on her finger. During a time of peace, it would have seemed to be a modest ring, but war made it an unexpected luxury. It was a real diamond set in real gold.

"Isn't it exciting?"

"It is. When will we see him again?"

"I'm not sure. His leaves keep changing, and they have him doing something special."

"Special?"

"Can't talk about it. Truth be told, I don't know the details; it's all rather mysterious. He has to keep secrets."

Anne said nothing in response. They both understood the word "special" and neither would hint at any knowledge of the meaning. It implied greater danger.

"He gave me this bracelet, too. Isn't it lovely?"

"Oooh, yes, it's quite delicate, though, so you'll have to take good care of it." Anne held Edith's forearm, while examining the bracelet. "I like those little paintings. Are these all things about Norway?"

"Yes. That's right." She smiled at Anne before adding "He told me he thought of giving me paper clips."

"Paper clips?" Anne raised her eyebrows. "There's nothing romantic about paper clips."

Edith laughed before replying, "That's what I thought at first, but I was wrong. People in Norway wear paper clips to defy the Nazis. It's a Norwegian thing. A Norwegian made the first paper clip, so it's all about national pride. The Nazis hate it."

"Ah, well I do like the bracelet, but the ring is the big thing. When will you tie the knot?"

"We don't know. We want to wait for the war to be over."

"Edie, the war might go on for a lot longer." Anne pointed out the obvious.

"Yes, but he wants to wait. He said he doesn't want to make me a widow."

"I don't like that thought." She frowned.

"What?" Edith smiled in response. "Does that mean you think I should be a widow?"

"Oh, tosh! Be off with you!"

"Good," was Peter's reaction when he saw the ring, "now she can never drag me off to any more dances!"

LONDON
1943

The uniform Terry Jones wore failed to give him the pleasure he had expected. He saw the way people looked at him while he rode his bicycle while wearing it. He also saw the way they looked at young men not much older than he was.

The older boys on the street, like Jack and Brian Harvey, Andy Lewis, and Jamie Gibson, were all seen as "men," while Terry Jones understood that he was still seen as a "boy." He wanted the transformation to happen quickly, but he had to wait until he was sixteen. As soon as that magical birthday came, he knew he could decide for himself and be seen as a man rather than a boy.

Mr. and Mrs. Jones were in the front parlour, with a pot of tea made of mint and roses, enjoying the flavour, even without sugar or milk or lemon. It was a time to relax and forget about the war, if only for the duration of a pot of tea.

They were drinking tea when Terry walked in, wearing his telegram boy uniform, and holding his head high.

"Hullo, lad, shouldn't you be at work?" his mum asked.

"Soon, but I'm here to tell you something else." He paused for effect. "I'm signing up."

"What!" His dad was the first to respond.

"You can't." His mum spoke firmly. "You've an important job right here!"

"I've done it, Mum. They want me back tomorrow."

"What about your job? Telegrams are important." Her voice was raised and tense, but Terry didn't notice.

"Billy Lee's got the job. He'll be using my bike."

"Why?"

"A soldier doesn't need a bike. That's for a boy like Billy."

***

The next day Billy Lee, wearing a telegram boy uniform, rode the same streets, riding the same bike Terry used. He had the same look of happy pride Terry had when he began. The first day was like Terry's, with some people happy to receive birthday wishes or congratulations, while others were anxious or greeted him with tears or screams. Going about His Majesty's business was not as he had thought it would be.

Like Terry Jones, Billy Lee became disillusioned with his uniform. He, too, noticed the way people looked at him when he rode his bicycle. He saw the women, like Anne and Mrs. Henderson, stop on their front paths, holding their handbags and shopping baskets, and the men, like Father, stopping on the pavement to watch. When he passed a pub, he knew the people in it were looking out at him, not touching their drinks.

"Not right, Mum," he said at the end of his first shift.

"There's nothing we can do," his mother explained. "You've a job to do and you just have to do it as best you can."

"I hate it."

"Yes, but there are more hateful jobs. All you can do is deliver the telegrams and say a little prayer for the people in the house.

LONDON
June 6, 1944

Mr. Jones pulled pints at the Rose and Crown, Millie Thompson played the piano, taking requests for favourite tunes, and other people played darts. Margie Denning no longer bothered to curl her hair or wear pretty frocks, and she had given up darts, losing interest when Billy Lee delivered a telegram about Harry Cummings. She came to the pub out of habit and sat watching the others at the dart board. Sometimes, they challenged her to play, but she always declined.

There had been rumours about changes, but no one knew what would happen. Everyone understood that loose lips sink ships, so they spoke in whispers about the possibility of a great invasion. The people at the Rose and Crown knew something would change, but they didn't know how. The only thing to do was go on as usual, with pints and songs and darts. The American, General Eisenhower, seemed to be on good terms with the prime minister and the King, and they seemed to trust him, despite his German name. There was little to do but wait.

While Mr. Jones was busy pulling pints and the people around Millie were singing, Billy Lee ran in, wearing his telegram boy uniform, and knocked over a table on his way into the pub. The pints of beer on the table spilled onto the patrons at the table and onto the floor. The men at that table stood up, angry at Billy. One of them reached toward the boy, ready to strike him.

"They've done it!" Billy called out to everyone in the pub. Millie stopped playing, and the patrons became silent.

The patrons who had lost their beer changed from anger to something else, something none of them could describe later.

"Done what, lad?" Mr. Jones deflected the potential anger of the men who had lost their beer.

"They've landed! It's the invasion!" the boy said in between gasps and could barely get it out.

"Tell us everything, lad," Mr. Jones insisted.

"That's all I know. It's all over the wireless. Our boys'll get old Adolf!"

One of the men who had lost his beer when Billy ran past called out, "This round's on me! A pint all 'round!" Everyone joined in singing when Millie played "Rule, Britannia!"

***

Harald's flights had taken him over France and Belgium and the Netherlands. His flights were direct, flying in straight lines from Beachy Head to assigned destinations. He could see details from the air. He could see beauty, but his assignment was always focused on the ugliness.

He could not think about the charm of rural places but had to consider whether there might be danger within the farmhouses or the barns. He had to ignore the details of beauty in haystacks and old villages and concentrate on the hard metal of railway lines and the specific locations of rivers and bridges.

On that day, Edith, Anne, and Father turned their thoughts to Peter. Perhaps he was thinking of an attractive redhead he had met the night Edith met Harald, but that was not a night when Peter could go dancing. He and thousands of other young men had been held in isolation from anyone outside their immediate military circles.

"On to France!" they shouted in small groups, each man wondering who would live and who would die.

The dangers were clear. Rommel had strengthened the Atlantic Wall, believing, correctly, that an invasion would come by way of the north of France and that it could be stopped only by stopping it at the beach. Concrete bunkers and pillboxes faced the sea, and the coast had been mined to prevent craft from landing. Everyone knew that many would not land and that those who did would have no cover.

Despite that, they sang "Roll Out the Barrel" and "Let's Hang Out the Washing on the Siegfried Line." Peter sang loudly, in his off-key voice, just as he would with a pint in a pub. Even while singing, he wondered which of his friends would live and which would die. He avoided contemplation of his own mortality.

American, British, and Canadian troops were sent across the Channel, most seasick long before landing, many sick with fear. The navies and air forces had been sent to support them by bombarding the coast in advance, attacking the bunkers and pillboxes and bombing supply routes. Commanders had studied the details of aerial photographs and were able to instruct the airmen exactly which bridges and roads to bomb to cut off supplies and reinforcements.

Although nominally "British," there were some air squadrons made up entirely of men from other countries—Poles, Czechs, Danes, Dutch, Norwegians, and others who fought for their own countries by fighting with the Allies.

Peter was with the troops who landed on Sword Beach. Other British units landed on Gold, the Canadians were on Juno, and the Americans climbed the cliffs at Omaha and Utah. The beaches were broad, extending for miles into the countryside, with no trees, no large rocks, and no cover other than the dead bodies of comrades. The cliffs were steep, as dangerous in themselves as guns at the top.

SWORD BEACH, NORMANDY
June 6, 1944

Peter had never seen such a broad beach. The ride over was rough, and he had slipped in other men's vomit as well as his own. The shooting began while they were still in the water. Wading in the sea made him think about paddling at the seaside as a child, but in those days, there had been no shooting, no smoke, and the sounds of sea birds instead of guns. The landing craft took them to a shallow place, where the sea met the land, and each wave changed the image of what was land and what was sea. Men around him fell, and he could do nothing but move on.

When he reached the place where the sea gave way to land, he dropped down and crawled, keeping as low and as flat as he could. There were few rocks, and no shelter from the bullets. He was torn between looking ahead to see what was next and keeping his face down, seeing only the sand beneath him.

The men followed orders because there was nothing else they could do. The noise of guns and aircraft obliterated spoken orders, so officers quickly gave their orders by hand signals, most as simple as a wave to the men behind them. Their men understood them instantly. Instant obedience had to come after the instant understanding so the time between the wave of an officer's hand and the forward movement of troops was momentary. Delay would result in death. Obedience would also result in death, but the orders could not be questioned.

The officers were the old men in the group, some as old as forty. Peter's captain was twice his own age. The captain led by example, moving ahead whenever there was a slight pause in the gunfire, and then moving ahead despite the gunfire. Perhaps it was because of the gunfire, as staying in one place made a man a still target. It was better to move, even in the direction of the guns.

Peter felt frozen to his place but looked up for guidance from his captain. Every wave of a hand gave him confidence. The men around him were the same, and all liked and trusted that leader. The noise was so intense that no one could hear words, but everyone understood the thoughts of the others. Peter ran and crawled along the beach, over the red stained uniforms of men who had preceded him onto the beach, and hid against them.

The guns were incessant, and Peter felt a need to pause. He had to take shelter, but there were no mounds of earth, so he took shelter behind his captain, grateful for the man's presence. When he looked up, he saw another officer wave to signal a move forward. Peter rose and obeyed the order, moving forward, and leaving the body of his captain where he had fallen.

LONDON
June 1944

Mrs. Harris liked to follow the rules but did occasionally slip a treat to a customer, especially if the customer had young children at home and a husband at the front. Her shop was the one Anne registered with because she liked Mrs. Harris and because it was close to the house. Having to register to use a shop was annoying, but it was the way rations were controlled. There were always women waiting to go in, holding their shopping baskets over one arm and clutching ration books in the opposite hand. Sometimes, the waiting would be dreary, especially when it rained or they had bad news from the front. When the news was good, there was a different feeling and the neighbours could chat and perhaps even share a laugh. The days after the invasion were strange. There was a feeling of hope, knowing that their troops were in France, but there was also anxiety about the young men they knew personally.

"Churchill has great praise for the generals." Mrs. Cooper smiled at Anne when she said it.

"He does, but it's our Peter I'm thinking about."

"When will you hear from him?"

"I don't know, and it wouldn't matter. I won't rest till he's home."

By the time Anne reached the fifth place from the shop door, the sky had become darker and the breeze had become wind. The ladies held their coats tightly, wanting to stay warm but unwilling to relinquish their places. Margaret Cooper was just ahead of Anne and Mildred West just behind her. The three chatted about their lads in France,

Churchill and the generals, and how small the rations were. Even if they had money, the amount of butter they could get on rations was small.

"My man's sick of ration recipes, and so am I," Mrs. West admitted.

"Aye, we all are," agreed the woman just behind her. "That carrot jam is all right, but I miss marmalade."

"My little lad needs more than just bits and bobs; he's growing."

"We can't all . . ."

The chat stopped when they saw Billy Lee. He rode by on his bike, wearing his telegram boy uniform. The women in the line stopped talking and looked up to watch Billy in silence. Everyone strained to see which house he would visit. When he turned off the street and was out of sight, they resumed taking as though they had never stopped, and as though they had nothing to fear from the sight of Billy Lee.

While Anne chatted with other ladies in the ration line, Edith met Harald in St. James' Park. They linked arms and strolled toward the bridge over the pond, while other couples linked arms in the same way or held hands or embraced—all in quietness. Everyone was in uniform, and most couples were in the same service. Edith and Harald served the air, but there were navy and army couples. The trees, the pond, the bridge, and the war formed their common backdrop.

"We're ever so worried about Peter. He's at Caen."

"Things are going well, but it's a slog."

"So, the newsreels are true?" She looked up at him, with hope in her eyes.

"As far as I can tell. The Yanks are advancing in Italy, and we're right across Normandy. It could still go pear shaped, but there's a lot more hope."

"What about Caen?"

"I can't lie to you, Edie. It's a tough battle."

"Do you think Peter will come home?"

"No one can say that about anyone. To say anything else to you would be a lie."

***

Flying Through the Ashes

In the days after the landings, Anne carried on as usual, sorting through her cupboards to see what was left and planning her use of ration coupons. She would make a list, as she always had, and decide which to choose first and when to go to the shop. The ration coupons allowed specific things, in amounts sufficient to maintain life, but she liked to save some to make special things as treats. She had learned when the queue was likely to be longer, and she also understood that being in a short queue might mean there was very little of whatever the people in it wanted. On the other hand, a long queue might mean the supply would end before the people at the end of the queue could move to the front.

After she had gone through her cupboards and made sure she had her ration coupons in her handbag, she would pick up her shopping basket and start down the front path. On a morning after the landings, she saw Billy Lee riding his bicycle, wearing his natty uniform, turning the corner onto her street.

Mrs. Anderson across the road was in the mirror position to Anne. Each woman held her handbag and shopping basket and stood completely still on her garden path. Each was aware of the other, but both were staring at Billy Lee. He came closer, and Anne and Mrs. Anderson both held their breath. Their houses were almost at the end of the street, and Billy Lee was not slowing down. Neither Anne nor Mrs. Anderson could take her eyes off Billy, who seemed larger than his physical size.

Then, while they were still holding their breath and when he started to get very close, he touched the pedal of his bicycle lightly to make it go more slowly. Anne and Mrs. Anderson both stiffened their bodies.

When Billy rode past, they relaxed and each took a deep breath and looked toward the other. Then they looked back toward Billy, who stopped his bicycle three doors down, on Mrs. Anderson's side of the road. It was the home of Mrs. Carson, who had been widowed when her husband failed to get to a shelter when he was on warden duty. Her son, Michael, was seventeen.

CAEN
June 1944

When the British and Canadian troops arrived in Caen, they were in a setting completely different from the beaches. Instead of the flat surfaces with no cover from guns, the city had small alleys and tight corners, making it impossible to see what might come next. No one could simply walk along a street; a soldier had to stay as close as possible to the walls, holding his back flat against the bricks while trying to see what was around the next corner or in the next alley.

There were places where fallen rubble made it impossible to stay near a wall, forcing the soldier out into the open of the street. Those were the most dangerous times. Once around a corner, English and German troops might meet each other face-to-face and then have to take the necessary next steps. Telegrams about Caen were sent frequently, delivered by boys in natty uniforms.

Peter moved into the city with his unit, watching his officers for their hand signals, giving orders, and watching the other men in his unit for theirs, giving warnings or "all clears." Being behind other soldiers made it less likely to be hit, but Peter felt guilty at that thought. Everyone in the group knew the others, and they had become best mates. That was as it had to be; they relied on each other for life itself. His guilt at feeling the safety of being one of those behind others made him move forward, even though no such order had been given. It was reckless, endangering the lives of others, as well as his own.

Peter moved forward, behind his lieutenant. The alley had been cleared of enemy soldiers and had been swept for mines. The officer had relied on the reports and deemed the position to be safe. They could move forward, although it wasn't clear why they were moving forward. Nor was it clear what they were moving into.

Caen's location, being a road hub and being at the place where the Orne River joins the Caen Canal, made it a crucial place to secure. In addition, the flat lands in the area were obvious choices for airfields. Commanders on both sides saw the importance of controlling this city, so the battle had to be fought hard. There would be casualties, but they were part of the unfortunate reality of a necessary battle.

Peter was senior in his small group of men, so he led the way into the alley. All remained wary, but they relied on the accuracy of previous intelligence reports.

Much of the old city no longer existed, even though it was there just days before. The streets were littered with the debris of a thousand years of history. The abbey survived, as did the castle, with the burial place of William the Conqueror, who had accomplished what Hitler hoped for.

Peter was oblivious to the history of the streets as he walked through the rubble. He and his small group of soldiers were the only people visible. They held themselves as flat as possible against whatever walls were still standing, avoiding the shattered glass on the ground and remaining silent, alert to the possibility of hidden enemies.

Peter led one group; his lieutenant led another. Peter looked across the street, watching for the lieutenant's signal. The signals were given by hand, in silence, but every man understood the meaning: *"We have to secure the bridge. You men, over there; you lot, follow me."*

In obedience to the hand signals, Peter and his group entered an alley while the lieutenant and four others moved toward a ditch. The ditch offered less cover for the men in it, while the buildings surrounding the alley offered more cover for the enemy. Each man kept his back as close to a wall as possible. Despite the sounds of gunfire, near and far, they were trapped in their own cocoon of silence.

Peter led his group through the alley and toward the bridge, and the lieutenant took his men to a shallow valley, more like a wide ditch,

Flying Through the Ashes

opposite them. Peter and the lieutenant looked at each other and the lieutenant gave a signal to move forward.

Peter could hear gunshots in the distance, but the alley he and his men had entered was completely quiet. After the noise of the beach and the fight to enter the city, the silence of the alley was overwhelming. No one in the group said anything, each man trying to silence his own breathing. It would have been helpful to have some reflective surface at the corners, to see what might be met, but there were only the matte surfaces of the stone walls and cobbled pavement.

Moving toward the bridge, they could see the others moving into the valley, with the lieutenant leading the way. There, too, it was silent. By that time, they were about one hundred yards apart, but it seemed that if one man whispered, those in the other group would hear him and whisper an answer.

The lieutenant looked back toward Peter and their eyes met. He nodded his head and moved his hand, gesturing they move forward in a new direction. Peter moved his hand to the men in his group, giving the matching order.

A noise. While they were moving toward the bridge, every man in the group noticed a pile of twigs that seemed to be moving. The lieutenant signalled them to stop and be silent. They held themselves still and silent; a moment of terror passed through them when the twigs moved again. At that moment, a rabbit jumped up from the twigs.

The men released their breath and smiled at each other and in the direction of the rabbit. They began to laugh. The laughter stopped when they heard a shot and their lieutenant fell. Miller, the next in command, took the lieutenant's group and the team returned to their mission.

"We have to keep going," Peter muttered to himself, knowing that every other man knew the same thing.

They noticed another pile of debris, apparently covering a human form in Luftwaffe uniform. Miller dragged himself toward it and poked it with a stick.

"Dead, poor fellow," he announced. "But what's he doing here? Right then, let's move forward."

When Miller was signalling the move, more gunfire began again. Miller fell, his face shattered. Peter looked down and saw blood soaking the front of his uniform.

LONDON
July 1944

Major Sutton's desk in the Cabinet War Rooms was at the edge of the corridor, with the back of his chair obstructing the entrance to an alcove with four other desks, but every part of the bunker was cramped, so it wasn't a slight. Being at the edge of the corridor made it possible for him to stand up whenever he pleased and move a few inches in any direction. His colleagues in the alcove had no such luxury.

Far from feeling slighted, he felt honoured to be there, so close to the decision makers. The prime minister himself had a small office and a small bed and had to pass the galley, as well as Major Sutton's desk, whenever he walked to the map room. Lack of any natural light kept the underground rooms in permanent night, the only reminder of time being the smells coming from the galley.

There was no privacy at the edge of the corridor, so Major Sutton always waited for busy times to retrieve his sugar. He kept a few cubes of it in his left drawer and used them sparingly. He had made a cup of tea and was just reaching toward the left drawer when a corporal approached.

"Sir," the corporal saluted, "news from France."

"Well, what is it?"

"We've taken Caen, sir. They're discussing it in the map room now."

"Caen? Bloody good! Did you hear that?" he shouted to the officers in the alcove. "We've taken Caen. They're discussing it in the map room now."

The other officers jumped up from their desks and pushed past Major Sutton so quickly that they didn't notice him move his sugar to the safety of his desk drawer.

The pins on the maps gave the prime minister, the Cabinet, and the military leaders the information they needed to make decisions about the conduct of the war. Within moments of becoming aware of movement of a front, staff would change the position of pins. The obvious problem was the need to become aware quickly. Positions could change with the fluidity of air, and there were days when pins moved back and forth across the map, forcing the decision makers to look beyond day-to-day strategy and toward the long term.

The long-term strategy was needed to win the war, but there were days, in the short term, when it meant larger loss of troops on the ground. The troops on the ground, like the units at Caen, had no individual knowledge of the long-term strategy or even of the short-term plans beyond those of their immediate officer's hand signals. They could do nothing but obey the hand signals.

***

Harald continued to fly and take photographs. While he flew, he could look down and see the details of the bodies still on the beaches, still in uniform, the fires started by bombs, the movement of troops across fields, and the wreckage left in villages invaded by opposing forces.

While he flew, guns were shot at Allied troops, at German troops, at buildings on the ground and planes in the air. He could see the faces of men firing at him. When a plane was hit, whether an ally or an enemy, the smoke began to pour from it while it still flew toward the place its pilot had aimed at. The plane, even in its dying moments, would continue to follow the orders until no longer capable. Then, whether quickly or slowly, the amount of smoke coming from it would increase, billowing in black clouds against the sky while the plane plummeted to a crash. If the pilot could eject, he would be part of the scene silhouetted against the sky, dangling from his open parachute, watching the death of his plane. Sometimes, the pilot's body could be seen from below, shocked by a bullet, and twisting in the throws of death. Other pilots, like Harald, could see all this but had to fly on.

Even while they flew, they understood the realities of losing control of their planes. Some pilots were able to eject and find safety behind barns or haystacks. Some remained in their planes while they burned. Those who survived might be captured by the Luftwaffe, who would follow the rules of the Geneva Conventions, or by the SS, who would not. A pilot in possession of a camera or film would be considered a spy and be detained by the Gestapo.

***

The family waited for news. Anne waited with other ladies waiting at Mrs. Harris's shop. Father waited with the patrons at the Rose and Crown. Even the children knew they were waiting for whatever would happen next.

News of the invasion had spread rapidly. No one had to wait any longer to learn when it would happen, or where. Instead, they waited for news of individual soldiers and sailors and airmen.

Anne and Father kept the radio on, listening to every word from the BBC. The prime minister continued to address the House of Commons, reporting on Allied success at Rome and the success of the storming of the coast of Normandy. He paid tribute to the generals, both in Italy and at the Channel, but everyone knew that the battles were fought by individual young men of all ranks. The prime minister referred to the advances that would have to be made over the next period of time. It was a warning that, even though the landings had been successful, fighting would continue. The telegram boys would continue to be busy.

Even though Edith was back at barracks, she waited for news in the same way as everyone else on her street. Anne and Father continued to watch Billy Lee as he rode his bicycle. The people in the pub continued to hold their pints silently watching to see where Billy might ride.

The battles, whether in Normandy or other parts of Europe or Asia or at sea, were still being fought. Days and nights went by when people knew who had received a telegram and who had not yet, but might still, receive one. Each day that ended without a visit from Billy Lee was a day of celebration. When a week went by with no one on the street seeing Billy, Anne and Mrs. Anderson knew what to do.

"Tea!" They agreed. The two women went out together, with their shopping baskets and saved ration coupons, and walked to the high street. One queued for tea and the other for butter. They had saved sugar.

They invited the ladies who lived on either side, and also invited Mrs. Carson and Mrs. Lindsay.

"Poor dears," Mrs. Anderson said. "That could be any of us. . . . They have to be included."

***

Billy Lee was busier than usual that month. The uniform was as natty as ever and service to the King was just as important, but he was always relieved when the day ended and he had no more telegrams to deliver.

Billy arranged his uniform more carefully than usual during that time. He brushed it every evening after his duty day and brushed it again the next morning, even though it had been set aside, unworn, after the previous brushing. He examined his hat every evening and every morning and brushed it at the same time he brushed the other parts of his uniform. Each time he examined the hat he gave the button at the top a little tug to make sure the thread was strong and the button was secure.

"Billy, I'm sorry you have to deliver this one," the lady at the telegram office told him. "But it's as it is, and it must be delivered."

Billy looked at the address.

"Are there others I can deliver first?"

"There are others, but this one has to be delivered, so you might as well get cracking and do it."

Billy took the telegrams, looked at himself in the looking glass, and adjusted his hat.

"You're dawdling. Just get going."

The uniform offered no reason to stay behind, and Billy understood that he, like the older boys in France, had to do his duty. Even so, he checked his bicycle and gave the metal an extra rub and cleaned off a few bits of imaginary soil.

"You're still dawdling." She had seen him from inside and came to the door. "I know how it is, lad, but delay won't help."

Billy nodded and started to ride, although more slowly than usual. He rode across the common, along the high street, and past St. Peter's Church, where he and the other boys had such fun making trouble for the vicar. Mr. Jones was unlocking the Rose and Crown when Billy rode by. Billy ignored his wave and pretended not to notice him. He had a specific address and a specific person to deliver to and he would not deviate from his instructions.

He continued the short distance past the Rose and Crown to the playground, and then on to the next street. He paused at the gate to the second house and leaned his bike against the hedge. It would have been easier for Billy if someone in the house had noticed him before he knocked, but that wasn't the case. He knocked and the door was opened by Mrs. Jones, who looked at him and collapsed against the door frame while her body heaved with sobs.

FRANCE
July 1944

The field hospital was, literally, in a field. Rain puddled on the canvas and caused the tent tops to bend inward. The rain and distant guns worked in cacophonous rhythm, sounds distracting from the smells of chloroform and blood and mud as doctors and nurses hovered over the wounded and tried to avoid the dead and dying. There was nothing to be done for them except cut off the duplicate ID tag that would give the information needed to send the telegram boys on their way. The other tag remained in place to ensure burial in the correct grave.

Peter could smell something. Rubbing alcohol? Latex? Dettol? Some strange blend of those and other, less recognizable things. There was no smell of dirt or gunpowder. His fingertips were on some smooth cloth, and even in semi-consciousness, he knew it was clean.

"Sir?" It was a woman's voice. "This one's coming around."

"Right then, let's have a look," a man answered. "Hello, there, laddie, can you hear me?"

Peter said nothing but felt his eyelids starting to flicker. Then they were far enough open for him to recognize the forms of a woman in the white uniform of a nursing sister and a man wearing a white jacket over some kind of military uniform. When his eyes were fully open, he looked directly at the man, who spoke to him.

"Narrow escape, lad, but you'll be all right. Can you tell me your name?"

He waited for an answer, but Peter was hesitant.

The man continued, "We're taking care of you. This is a British hospital. . . . A cool cloth, nurse."

The woman placed a damp cloth on his forehead. The wet coolness moved him closer to full awareness.

"Can you give us your name?" the man asked again.

"Name and rank and number and nothing else until I know who you are."

"Good, lad." The doctor and nurse both smiled. "It sounds as though you're all there. You've had a rough time. We did a bit of surgery, but you'll be all right."

"My mates?" Peter wanted to know. "The others?"

The nurse turned her attention to a tray on the bedside table, and the doctor hesitated before putting on a smile and answering with, "No details right now. It's you we're working on."

Neither of them could lie well.

LONDON
July 1944

"*We'll meet again. Don't know where, don't know when, but I know we'll meet again some sunny day . . .*" Vera Lynn sang the promise to everyone who listened to the radio, and that was everyone in the country. The promise came in song, along with that of bluebirds over the white cliffs of Dover. The promise of meeting again was usually met after arrangements made by letter. Sending a telegram, even with happy news, could be cruel to the recipient, who would suspect the worst when opening the door to a telegram boy.

Harald and Edith had exchanged letters before the bombing of Wellington Barracks. They routinely met in the chapel there, assuming it would always be available. Then, one day, a bomb fell directly on the chapel. They had a date and time, so each went to the usual place, as though nothing had changed. They hugged and kissed, despite the ruins around them and the smell of high explosive mixed with dust and dirt and death.

"Caen?" he asked after the kiss.

"Good news! He's been wounded!"

"How badly?"

"Nothing missing, but he has to mend."

"So, he's coming home?"

"Yes."

"Thank God for being wounded!"

"I don't know what think. He's alive now, but they want to send him back into action. I wish he were wounded more badly. It's horrid.

They're fixing him up but might send him back to get shot at again." She hesitated. "Do they really do that?"

"Send men back? Yes, if they are fit enough." He paused. "You never know what will happen next, even after being wounded."

"I hope the wound is more serious than he said." She understood the irony in her comment, even as she made it. "If they send him back, I hope he's wounded again and I hope it's more serious."

"No, Edie, never wish for things like that."

They exchanged no more words but simply held hands and walked across the road to the park. They were an air force couple, strolling in the presence of navy couples, army couples, Americans, Canadians, Poles, Czechs, and rich and poor. St. James' Park was the place of reunions, where lovers walked hand in hand, exchanging news about friends and family or simply remaining silent.

BAVARIA
1944

"Frau Meier." The butcher smiled. "We have fine sausages today. . . . We are fortunate."

"Danke," she replied, not wanting to ask the price. She knew how much money she had and how long it had to last, but the sausages did tempt her. "Two, then," she decided.

While she walked back through the village, she thought of how shameful her life had become. Her husband had found work at another farm, mucking another farmer's barn, but there was little money. She thought about all the time he wasted potting plants in his shed. She saw no reason to pot plants; instead, she planted vegetables directly in the soil. Without her efforts, they would have barely anything to eat. The meagre income Konrad had from the farmer was little more than the price of the flour she used to make bread. It was all so humiliating. The other women in the village were proud of their husbands and sons, and let her know it.

"My Manfried is in Paris," Frau Zweig said, with a snide smile. "He writes to me about the Eiffel Tower and the great churches. It has been good for him, but he is anxious to be off fighting on the front."

Marta Meier had no way to reply to such comments. Many of the husbands, and most of the sons, were in uniform. Some were in the Luftwaffe, some in the army, some in the SS, and the wives and mothers kept the photos of uniformed men on tables in their front rooms.

"I'll eat the sausages myself," Marta decided when she returned to her kitchen. "I am the one who is making an effort for this war. . . . He deserves nothing."

She cooked both sausages, ate one, and set the other aside for later. Even as she did it, thinking she would eat it herself, she wondered whether she might relent and give it to her husband. After all, he did have the job at the farm, even though it was so much less than he could have been if he had just accepted a uniform.

She cleaned her tables, swept the floor, and polished the windows. When the sun went down, she wondered where her husband was. He should have left the farm and been home by then.

To not even tell me! she thought. *No, I won't give him the sausage!*

"Konrad," she called, and then went out to look for him.

She found him suspended from a beam in the garden shed.

LONDON, 1944

Anne relaxed with her knitting, Father with his pipe, and Edith with a game of Patience. It was a quiet day, with the music on the BBC interrupted only by welcome news about the action at the front. The war was changing, and the family adjusted to the changes.

Jimmy was in the front room when he heard the gate open. He looked past the blackout cloth to see who it might be. He knew the boy. He was a bit older and was much better at football. He wasn't one of his usual friends, though, being just a bit too old for that.

"Mummy?" Jimmy called. "Why is Billy Lee here?"

When Anne heard the question, she gasped. "Is he in his uniform?"

"You mean the thing he wears with the silly hat?"

"Yes, darling . . . is he in that?"

"Yes. Mum, but he's coming up the path. . . . Why is he here?"

Anne couldn't answer but went to the door with the same question in her mind. She waited at the door, standing inside, doing the expected thing of allowing the person on the other side to knock before she opened the door, even though she wanted to open it while he was still walking up the path.

He knocked. She opened.

"Terribly sorry, ma'am," the boy mumbled. He knew what it was, but he didn't know what to say. He never did, despite all the times of practice.

Oh, no, Anne thought when she saw the name on the telegram.

Edith was still playing Patience when Anne walked in.

"Edie, this one is for you."

Edith took the telegram but did not open it. She removed her ring, placed it on the mantle, and left the room.

PART TWO
THE VIEW FROM AKASHA

The end of the war meant parties and celebrations, but it also meant memories of all that had been lost. Edith continued to wear the bracelet Harald had given her when he gave her the ring. Very few people, only her family and closest friends, knew the history of the bracelet, and she didn't want sympathy from people who were unrelated, so she usually avoided questions by keeping it hidden beneath her sleeve.

Still in uniform, she was a serving member of the military for another two years. Those years were spent in Berlin, as a member of the Allied Occupying Forces. She served in an ordinary position, which would have been boring in civilian life. Reports had to be typed and filed, and men had to be the ones in charge, too proud for women's work. The women shared barracks. Not all were of the same background, but Lady Julia was never addressed as "My Lady" and never expected it.

They lived in a large house, with vines that were once beautiful but had grown across the windows, obstructing the view. The path crossed an area with remnants of a garden, and Edith recognized the fragrance of the roses she had enjoyed before the war. The house had shingles that reminded her of large English country houses, and a large reception hall. It was formerly the home of a senior officer who had served the Reich. The pictures of that of officer and his family, and Hitler, had been replaced by pictures of the King and notice boards giving information to the new occupants.

Despite being in the uniform of the enemy occupier, Edith was invited to the homes of local people. They reminded her of the people on her own street.

Going home was impossible, as home as it had been no longer existed. St. Paul's was as magnificent as ever, but the area around it was rubble. Her own street had been spared, but many houses were in mourning and always would be. Most importantly, she could no longer enjoy St. James' Park, or Lyons Corner House. London was no longer her home.

Harald had told her about his time on Toronto Island and the welcome he had received from the people. The trainees were busy, but every flight took them up over the island and the lake, and while learning to manoeuvre their own planes, they watched others flying in formation against dawn or sunset over Lake Ontario.

She had nothing left of Harald except for memories and the bracelet. Seeing Toronto, with its island park and harbour, seemed appropriate, so she booked passage on a ship. She didn't know what to expect in Toronto but discovered that she could still go dancing. She bought new dance dresses and went to a place overlooking the lake. The music was the same as in England, and it was a good way to meet Canadians. She married one of them and settled into life as a housewife in a small Canadian town.

Everyone in her town went to church every Sunday, including her mother-in-law, who lived next door. The family expected it of Edith, but defended her when people in town noticed that she didn't bother to attend Sunday services. It was only slightly less embarrassing to them than if she had been a Catholic. The shops were as they had been in London before the war, with friendly people and no ration books. The people were kind to her but ostracized another woman.

Edith met Bruni when she bumped her grocery cart. Mrs. Brown, at the cash register, saw it happen.

"You! You did that on purpose!" Mrs. Brown gestured toward Bruni's cart.

"No, I bumped her, and I'm sorry," Edith responded while Bruni remained silent.

"No! She did it, and we don't want her kind. We fought the damn krauts, and then they come over here and expect they can bash our grocery carts. She should damn well go back where she came from."

Other women in the store watched and nodded in agreement with Mrs. Brown while Bruni remained silent.

"She's right," Mrs. Carter said. "My Andy was shot down by the bloody Luftwaffe, and now the krauts come here and expect to live with us."

"And now we're finding out what they did to the Jews!"

"Well, we don't want Jews here, either, do we?"

Other women watched, most remaining in place and silent, nodding almost imperceptibly. Edith and Bruni both blushed, paid for the few things they had gathered, and left together.

"I am very sorry about that." Edith knew it was her cart that had hit Bruni's.

"Oh, it was my fault. I must be more careful." Bruni wanted to take responsibility in response to kindness.

"They don't know what it was like. Where are you from?"

"Bavaria, and you?"

"London. We must have coffee. Would you like to come to my house?"

That was the first day of coffee for the two of them. Each had been in military service, Edith under Churchill and Bruni under Hitler. They were both married to Canadians and had children the same age. The children grew up, but the coffee continued.

TORONTO
1969

"Ach, I remember what we called coffee in those days." Bruni laughed.

"And tea! Remember the linden buds? Not quite the same as tea leaves, were they?"

Edith and Bruni spent summer afternoons that way, sitting on the porch, drinking iced coffee and reminiscing. Those afternoons usually ended in giggles.

"Oh, the officers—there was one group captain who looked like Cary Grant!"

"Ach, yes, we had a hauptmann who was like Hercules!"

The two of them—the Englishwoman and the German—giggled while remembering officers. One retained her London accent; the other spoke English with the lilt of Bavaria.

"Ah, Lovely Larry . . . that's what we girls called him . . . he was Sir Lawrence something, but we called him Lovely Larry. Not to his face of course! We all knew he had a countess waiting at home."

"Ach, we had the same. . . . Whenever there was a 'von' in the name, the officer had better looks! I always wanted to serve under the vons! Hercules was a 'von,' but there was a baroness for him."

"Did you ever get caught out after curfew with a von?"

"Oh, how I wish I had! No, the only ones I was caught with had no von at all."

The two kept pausing and giggling. They even giggled about air raids.

"Remember getting drinks mixed up?"

"Ach! Yes! When all the lights went off and we had to hide under tables! Yes, we got drinks mixed up and kept sipping each other's. . . . We had to watch the ones who wanted to take gulps of everyone else's during the dark!"

"The wardens in London were lovely . . . always told me to get on to a shelter, but they were all right. Same thing with the policemen."

"Things were different for us with the people in charge. Arrogant Nazis . . . we didn't like them any more than you did. Before the war, my village had a nice policeman, but then . . . . well, things changed."

"The policemen who know you are always the best. We had lots of bobbies in London, but there was always the local one and he was always the one who caught the boys scrumping apples."

"We had one of those when I was a child. He kept my brother away from the neighbour's apples, but he never suspected me. He didn't think a girl would climb a tree! Ach, yes, I remember that man."

The two friends paused, each thinking of policemen they had known as children.

"What about Lovely Larry?" Bruni asked. "Did he marry the countess?"

"No. No, poor old Larry didn't make it . . . not anything dramatic. It was a bombing raid. What about Hercules?"

"Not so lucky as Lovely Larry. He was captured and sent east. That was far worse than a bomb."

"Ah, so the baroness was as heartbroken as the countess."

"The baroness did all right. She met an American during the occupation."

"Right then. The Yanks and the baronesses made it through!"

Then they knocked back more iced coffee.

The two friends were still sitting on the front porch, sipping coffee and enjoying the garden, when a red Volkswagen arrived and parked in front of the house. Two young people, both with long hair and beaded headbands, got out. The girl wore a long floral skirt and peasant blouse, and her friend wore a torn jacket and jeans.

"Is that Sarah?" Bruni asked. "She looks so different."

"Yes, but they all look strange these days. I try not to say anything or she'd just be worse."

"Hi, Mum, hi, Bruni," Sarah greeted them. "Mum, you know Roger. Roger, this is Mum's friend, Bruni."

"A pleasure to meet you." Bruni shook his hand. "I have heard about you."

"So, what are you two doing today?" Edith asked.

"University Avenue," Sarah answered without explanation, knowing her mother would understand.

"There's a march past the American consulate," Roger explained to Bruni.

"About Vietnam?" Bruni understood.

"Yes."

"But it isn't your war," Edith interrupted.

"That's what I keep telling him," Sarah added.

"It's everybody's war." Roger spoke softly.

"I agree with you, young man," Bruni said. "And I agree with your protest. I grew up in a place where we could not do such things. Be glad you can go on this march, and do so with my blessing."

"Blessing?" Edith asked. "You use that word?"

"Yes, from the war. We looked for blessings. I didn't like church, but I prayed."

"So why didn't you go to church?" Sarah asked.

"Oh, a lot of reasons. There were good priests, but the bravest and best were taken away. In my little place, we didn't know what to feel when we heard the prayer with 'Dein Reich Komme.'"

Edith liked to go to church on Christmas Eve to hear the carols, but that was the extent of her involvement with organized religion. She did admit that she had prayed.

"I'm not much for prayer," Edith said "but when those bombs were falling I prayed . . . oh, yes, I prayed!"

"When else?" Sarah asked.

"Oh, when you know people on your street will die, when you know the boys are over the Channel or off in France, or on the sea. . . .

There were a lot of times there's not much else to do but pray and have a cigarette or go off to a dance."

"Cigarette?" Sarah raised her eyebrows.

"Yes, on my doctor's advice."

"What?"

"In those days, all the doctors told us there was nothing for it but to have a cigarette and a cup of tea when the bombs were falling."

"So, it was your doctor who got you smoking?"

"Yes, and all the doctors smoked, too, so don't start criticizing me for it!"

"Ach, yes!" Bruni nodded, and waved a cigarette of her own.

***

Iconic photos of the Vietnam War spread quickly: a young girl running naked along a street after a napalm attack, helicopters in mass force, people taking refuge in streams, a man pointing a gun at another man's head and looking as though he would enjoy shooting the man who is bound and whose face reveals his fear. These were the photos a generation knew, and they marched. They marched, in long skirts and jeans and jean jackets, and carried signs and listened to Joan Baez and Jane Fonda.

For Americans, it was personal. In Canada, it was different. Roger could not be conscripted. Sarah did not fear widowhood at the age of twenty. They did not hear taps played at local cemeteries. Some Canadians voluntarily joined the American army and fought in Vietnam, but for them it was a personal choice rather than a draft notice.

There were demonstrations across the world, most of them in the USA, a country torn by war, even though the war was on another continent. Men who had landed on the beaches of Normandy or on the coast of Italy, or who had been tortured in the South Pacific, had seen friends die suddenly and had struggled over the words to write to young widows or middle-aged mothers. Many of the men who had experienced those things were proud of sons who were fighting, just as they had been proud of their own fathers, who had fought in an earlier war.

Other men had other feelings. News that a son had evaded the draft or deserted his post challenged emotions. Fathers and mothers wanted their sons to be safe, but for many it was a matter of honour. Fathers and sons disagreed, and husbands and wives argued. Sometimes, the husband wanted his son to follow in his own footsteps, to place his medals side by side with his above the mantle. In other homes, the mothers wanted the sons to make the family prouder while the fathers thought back to the smell of blood mixed with saltwater mud.

Many of the young men who evaded the draft or deserted military service fled north, to Canada, where people their own age lived in innocence and had no fear of death in a faraway land. Those Canadians who did go south joined the American military to fight in what their parents saw as another country's war.

Every university in Canada had demonstrations, with professors and students walking side by side, carrying signs opposing the war and singing the songs of their era.

Toronto was the largest city in Canada. Young people from many parts of the country left their classes and gathered there. Roger and Sarah were among the lucky ones who already had a comfortable place to sleep, unlike those who risked sleeping on the lawns of public buildings. Roger's friend, Ken, joined them, miraculously able to find them in the crowd at the legislature.

"I have signs for you." Ken had no other greeting. "We go down University Avenue, right by the American consulate, and end at City Hall. It should get lots of press."

Ken led Roger and Sarah to a position at the front of a column of people.

"I'm putting you in charge. You're the best guy to keep it all together. Remember to make them stay on pace, not too fast and not too slow, and you lead the chants. You can decide which ones to use, but we want it as uniform as possible."

Ken was a deserter from the American army and had spent six months in Vietnam. He would never forget being on a hill, shooting down at people who were shooting back at him, and the guy on his left was shot a moment before the guy on his right. At that moment Ken decided to go AWOL the next time he was on leave. He was from a small town in the American Midwest, an only son. His parents flew the flag from their front porch and never missed a Fourth of July celebration. His father's medals from World War Two were displayed on the wall of the front room, beside his grandfather's from World War One. His Uncle Joe had his medals, speaking of action in Italy, above the mantle in his front foyer, along with those of his great-uncle, who went missing in France. Uncle Joe never missed a chance to mention that his son, Joe Junior, was in the Marines, serving in Vietnam.

"Remember to meet me tonight. We'll need to plan the next one, and I want to get the key people together."

"Right," Roger answered, not noticing Sarah's expression.

She didn't speak to him until Ken had left and they had left the lawn of the legislature. "Why didn't you check with me?"

"What do you mean?"

"You keep going along with anything Ken asks, and it's like I'm your pet dog."

"Ah, nice puppy." He tried a smile. "Why the growl?"

"Don't ever do that again! I'm going along with this, but you have to at least let me know what's going on and you have to make sure I'm ok with it."

"Ok. I apologize."

They started down the Avenue, chanting with everyone around them and angling the signs toward television cameras. Everyone stayed in unison, and no one stepped out of the columns, so it was easy. There were doctors and nurses on smoke breaks in front of the hospitals and lawyers in barristers' gowns watching from the sidewalk beside Osgoode Hall. Most of them nodded, and some clapped and cheered. There were guards in front of the American consulate, but no one broke out of line, so the guards were just observers.

"When this is over, I'd like to relax." Sarah was tired, but she didn't want to admit it to Roger. She couldn't let him see her lack of enthusiasm.

"It won't be over for a long time. Years."

"You know what I mean."

"Right." Roger felt slightly guilty. "Let's do something special."

"What?"

"Let me surprise you." His eyes sparkled with energy. "My grandfather wanted to celebrate my birthday. It's a big deal for him."

"I don't get it. Why such a big deal?"

"He's all about the old thing about turning twenty-one." He shrugged his shoulders. "I'm the only grandson and he has a thing about boys carrying on the family name."

"He sounds like an old grump."

"No, you'd like him."

She frowned in reply. "It sounds to me like he has a big thing for the boys, but girls don't count." She waited for a response. When none came, her curiosity forced her to go on. "So, what is this thing?"

"You know Grandpa paid for my PPL, right?"

"Your what?"

"Private pilot's license." He said it quietly, but she knew he wanted to call it out to the world.

"What about it?"

He smiled and shook his head, putting a finger over his lips.

When the march was over, Sarah sat at the edge of the reflecting pool at City Hall, watching Roger take their signs to a collection area and speak to Ken. She saw them looking back at her, and then Roger came to her with a smile.

"Ok, let's go."

"Where?"

"Trust me." His smile did not comfort her. She wanted an answer.

He led her to the subway station, and the two took a train to Union Station. "This is our stop. From here, we walk."

"Are we going to the Island?"

"Yes."

It wasn't until she saw a small plane flying overhead that she understood. Roger was taking her to another part of the Island rather than to the ferry docks. It was the Island airport, and when they arrived, he pointed to a small plane.

"Here we are. You wait here while I do some checks." He tried to avoid showing his excitement.

"Is it yours?" Her eyes were wide open.

"Yep. Do you want to go up?"

"What a question! Of course, I want to go up! I've never been in one of those."

***

Flying was about fun. While circling the Toronto Islands, watching boats sailing to and from the yacht club, they were oblivious to their American contemporaries, who were flying other planes half a world away. Serious as they looked and felt while carrying signs outside the consulate, war was part of other people's lives.

"This airport is old," he told her while helping her into the plane. "The Norwegians used it for training."

"Norwegians? When?"

"World War Two. They had their barracks over there, in Little Norway Park. A lot of those guys flew with the RAF."

He took her up and out over the lake, circling the islands and skimming the edges of the city. They flew over the parks and over the suburbs, watching people playing golf and children swimming. They saw cyclists on the paths beside rivers and families having picnics. Circling the islands, they saw the glitter of sunlight on waves and watched mothers caring for children on the beaches. The ferries moved, in a pattern like a dance, between the mainland docks and the three ferry docks on the islands. It was a place where war could be forgotten and the flyers could remain oblivious to the wrecks of schooners and loss of children in storms that marked the history of the south shore.

"I love Akasha," Roger stroked the yoke of the plane.

"Akasha?"

"That's what I call her."

"Her? Is this plane female?"

"Don't worry; it's a compliment."

"What does it mean?"

"It's Sanskrit. It means open air, ether, space, all in a mystical sense. Akasha takes me up into freedom."

"Not if you crash."

"I'll never crash. Akasha won't let me."

He laughed, and she laughed with him. The lake was calm, and the sky was blue on blue, open and clear, above the blue on blue of the lake; the darkest blue marked their division.

"Look! Look over there!" Sarah pointed. "The horizon line really is a line. It's a different blue from the water or the sky."

"That's how it is today, and that's good."

"Look at those boats! They're right on the horizon line."

"They're on our horizon line, but they have horizons of their own," he said softly.

"What do you mean?"

"They see other horizons. They can't see ours, and we can't see theirs. Sometimes, you can't see a horizon line at all. When no one sees a horizon line, it's a really bad day." His voice was almost imperceptible.

They continued to fly over the lake and the Island and the mainland. They saw residential neighbourhoods where men were working on cars, women were cutting flowers or raking their gardens, and children were playing on swing sets.

***

While Roger and Sarah carried signs along University Avenue, from Queen's Park, past the American consulate, they would talk about other things. They chanted the chants, along with everyone else but found time for picnics on Toronto Island or flights over Niagara Falls.

Trips over Niagara had special excitement. He was careful to avoid flying into American airspace, despite the temptation to do so. From the air, there appeared to be no difference between the two countries. In that area, they were not even "north" or "south" of each other, as the forces of nature changed the angle of a political border.

They had American friends who were given A's in all their university courses by professors intent on preventing them from being drafted.

Others had come north as draft dodgers or deserters and could not return to their own country.

Roger was in no such danger and felt embarrassed and slightly guilty when meeting those Americans. The days of flying were an escape, an escape from guilt felt at being safe while their friends were not.

His plane was a Cessna 172. If he ever wondered about the cost of fuel, he didn't show it while in the air. Sarah didn't think about it at all. They simply got into the plane and then soared. He liked to circle the Island after takeoff, and then circle the city and go farther afield.

"That's Holland Marsh," he might point out or, "That's the Lake Simcoe Yacht Club."

Flying over Niagara Falls seemed mildly daredevil, and there was something wonderful about those daredevil days.

"Bring your camera," Roger would often suggest.

They could get great shots of life on the ground. He flew, and she clicked the camera, but he was always making suggestions: "Over there—take one of that train" or "that would be a good shot . . . that man on the horse" or "look at the way the sunset outlines that building."

When they developed the photographs, they saw things they had not noticed from the air. While flying, they were moving, but the printed pictures were still, allowing time to notice fine points.

"Oh, look at that," Sarah said, pointing toward the corner of one picture. "His trousers are falling down!"

***

November brought another wave of intensity, of a different kind. Exams were coming and term papers were due. Roger and Sarah spent more time in the library than anywhere else but still went to the Island occasionally for the pleasure of flying. The air was colder and denser, so Akasha took off without effort and soared.

The scenery below changed from the summer days of golf and swimming to the changes of leaves, from dark green to yellow and orange and red, giving way to bare branches and the occasional skim of sparkling frost.

Flying Through the Ashes

Roger and Sarah were in the library, cramming for exams, when Ken approached.

"News," he said, offending Sarah by addressing Roger instead of the two equally.

Neither said anything but looked at Ken with eyes wide open, waiting for his next comment.

"News. Shit from 'Nam. Shit like you wouldn't believe." He paused, but neither Roger nor Sarah responded, neither knowing what to say. "There was a little village, called My Lai. Some crazy bunch of Americans went in and killed them all. Just went nuts. No reason. Just nuts."

"What do you mean by 'all'?" Roger asked.

"All means all. The whole village."

"Who took the children?" Sarah wondered.

"Dead. Like I said, all means all. Even babies. They just …"

"That can't be true," Sarah interrupted. "Americans would never do that."

Roger and Ken glared at her.

At first, they couldn't believe it. American soldiers had gone into a small village and slaughtered the inhabitants. There had been orders to kill all Viet Cong, including women. The dead at My Lai included babies. The victims ranged from infancy to people in their eighties. One soldier would later comment that his opinion was that the soldiers in his platoon didn't consider the Vietnamese human. It seemed impossible, and at first, many people thought it was someone's sick idea of a joke or some extremist lie.

Roger and Sarah, and all their friends, were stunned by the news. Then they became angry. Roger was furious. He had always been cautious about language while with Sarah, but when they realized that My Lai had happened, he used language she had never heard him use before. He and Ken called the usual people and made more than the usual plans. Rallies and demonstrations took place all over the world, but Roger and Ken would be key organizers of the local ones.

A few days later, Roger and Sarah were at the legislature again, carrying signs and signing chants.

"There's nothing you can do to change it," Sarah commented. "You can carry your signs and walk as far as you want, but you won't change a thing."

"So, we should do nothing?"

"I don't know what to do."

"We don't know what difference we can make, but we won't change things if we don't try. We all have to do our bit."

"Why isn't Ken doing his bit?"

"What?"

"He's an American. Why is he here? Why isn't he fighting for his country?"

"You just don't get it, do you?"

"What you don't get is that it isn't our war." She was annoyed with him but still wanted to be with him. His insistence on taking part in demonstrations made her feel that she couldn't avoid taking part. He insisted on going, and she wanted to be with him.

"Wrong. It's everybody's war." He was emphatic. "Your mum's friend, Bruni, gets that."

"Don't start talking to me about Bruni. That was another time."

"Yes, and things became so bad that people like her had no way to deal with the things they had thrown at them. We have to deal with the things we can, the things in our own time."

"As soon as this is over, I want to get back to the library. We have semi-finals coming up." She felt it better to change the topic.

"I have another idea. I know you didn't want to be in this Let me make it up to you."

***

He took her back to Akasha, and they soared together. Akasha flew, as if by magic, over the changing shades of blue of the lake, the browns and greys of the land, and the dark greens of the pine woods to a cloud of pale grey mist rising above Niagara Falls. There were rainbows over the fields and the woods and the river separating two countries. American and Canadian flags flew on the bridges, and all seemed calm.

"Oh, look at those gardens!" Sarah saw the bright colours of pumpkins and corn stalks and leaves. "Can we fly over there?"

"No, that's in the States."

"We wouldn't land," she pleaded. "I just want a closer look." She was excited about the beauty on the other side of the river.

"No way. Just reach for the binoculars."

Flying released them from care. Akasha took them up to a place where they could see the details of daily life, as though the houses and cars and people were toys.

***

Christmas exams were as usual, and the Christmas break was as welcome as always. Roger invited Ken to spend the break with him, and Sarah went home to her parents. Ken was unsure about whether to call his family but decided to do so. Roger and Ken spent the next morning playing cards. Ken won three games.

"Damn. You have all the luck." Roger grimaced when he saw the cards.

"Maybe in this but not much else." Ken was distracted, and the card game did not help.

"News? You didn't say anything about that phone call."

"Bad. My cousin's coming home in a box."

"Your dad's nephew?"

"Yep. My uncle and aunt are acting like it's all my fault. Mom didn't say it, but I'll bet my dad feels that way, too."

"Like you could stop a war?"

"Yep."

"Isn't that what you're trying to do?"

"Not in their minds. My dad and most of the family think I'm a traitor. My mom and my sister probably just don't talk about me. They're ashamed of me, too."

"Did you talk to him on the phone?"

"No, Mom answered. At least she didn't hang up."

"Would your dad?"

"He has before and it's worse with that funeral coming up."

"Call him again and speak to him." Roger spoke softly to Ken, realizing that he was on the brink of tears.

"No point in trying. He was one of the good guys on D-Day. Landed on the beach, went on, and fought. All that stuff."

"This is different."

"You can't tell them that. Joey's getting the full military funeral: the brass, the folded flag, the whole bit . . ." Ken paused and looked down at his cards, "and my parents and sister will be there and everybody in town will be looking at them and thinking about me, and about where I am and where they think I should be."

***

University life returned to normal in January. Students hurried from one building to another, less worried about being late for a class than about avoiding the cold wind between buildings. Pulling scarves over their faces was ineffective against the cold when moisture from their breath froze and stiffened the fabric.

"Guys like Ken, good guys, can't even visit their parents, and guys like his cousin, other good guys, will never do anything again. . . . There's just so much about this damn war." Roger slammed his fist against a glass table in the study room, fracturing a bone at the side of his right hand and almost hitting Sarah. "This goes beyond shit!"

"You nearly broke that glass."

"I might have broken something else." He cradled his injured hand in the other.

Sarah was disdainful of the foolishness of hitting hard glass but took pity on Roger, who was humiliated by his own action. She took him to the emergency room and waited with him while the day changed to evening and then to night. They could hear the sounds of ambulances getting louder as they approached, and the rhythm of steps of medical staff in the halls nearby. When Roger's name was called they were guided to a pale green cubicle.

While in the waiting room at Toronto General, waiting for X-ray results, he continued to fume about My Lai and about Vietnam generally.

"Assholes!" he said it aloud while a doctor was examining his hand. When the doctor pulled his head back and stared at him, Roger realized his mistake.

"Oh, sorry . . . it's just all this stuff we keep hearing."

The doctor raised his eyebrows.

"I know it sounds stupid, but it's just all this stuff we keep hearing about Vietnam."

"Why take it out on a table?"

"It really gets to me."

"Yes, it is terrible. Let's be glad it doesn't involve any of us."

Sarah watched Roger stiffen and was relieved when he didn't reply.

When they left Toronto General, his right hand was in a splint, so they held hands with her right and his left and walked along the grass on the median of University Avenue. They walked south, toward the American consulate, so she knew she had to divert his attention.

"Can you still fly?" she asked, gesturing toward the splinted hand.

"Sure. Why not?"

"I just wondered about holding controls."

"Is that a challenge?"

"Not really, but this is a beautiful night."

"You might have to help me a bit."

"What? I don't know how to do anything in a plane. We'd crash." She knew he used his right hand when flying.

"Just do what I tell you." His confidence was contagious, but she still had doubts.

They went down to the Island and up into the air. A night flight revealed other details: city lights reflecting on the surface of the lake and areas of darkness on the south side of the Island. He showed her which dials to turn and where to set them. He was able to handle everything else.

***

Back at university again, Roger was still embarrassed about the injury to his hand. "Guys in the States coming back with no legs or eyes or arms and I'm messing around with a finger bone!"

"Yeah, well that finger bone is going to mess up your life if you don't talk to your profs!"

"It's stupid! A finger bone!" he growled.

Writing an examination would be more challenging than usual. He caved in and talked to the profs. They were sympathetic, with comments like, "Too bad you didn't smash it on Nixon's head," and in each case, he was allowed to either do an oral exam or get a deferral. Despite his self-inflicted injury, he maintained his average and it didn't interfere with flying.

They were in a study hall when they heard about Kent State. Students, protesting in the same way they did, were killed by their own people. The newspaper showed a photo of a young woman, wearing the same styles of clothing and hair as most of their friends. In the photo, she was holding her arms out, leaning over the body of another student, her mouth open in a scream. Looking at the photo, they could hear the scream. It was in someone else's country, and yet so close.

Universities in the United States went into deep mourning for the four who were killed and for the condition of their country. Students went on strike, insisting on their right to protest in safety. Young American men continued to come north to the mixed feelings of their families. To some, they were traitors; to others, refugees.

At the rallies and marches, Roger and Sarah would walk, carrying the usual signs and singing the songs written by the music icons of their day. There was always someone with a guitar to lead the group in "If I Had a Hammer" or "Blowing in the Wind": *". . . how many times can a man turn his head, and pretend he just doesn't see? The answer, my friend, is blowin' in the wind . . ."*

They always felt tense after a rally or a march. Roger was in no danger, but their American friends could not return to their own country. They didn't know what to say to them. After the rallies and marches, they went down to the Island, to Akasha, and went flying.

The flying days were always clear and sunny, with the lake sparkling beneath, the shadow of the plane on the ripples. They would fly over and around the islands, watching the sailboats and the cyclists. Then they would fly farther out and see the tiny details of other people's lives. There were so many details: a woman cutting flowers in her garden, a man working on his car, children playing on swing sets, a couple holding hands while walking in a park.

Flying raised their spirits and helped them forget the details of other people and other places. It always seemed to be summer when they flew, and the summer seemed eternal, no matter what the month.

Roger didn't usually take anyone else up in Akasha, but he would sometimes take Ken.

"I couldn't get her," Ken announced one evening, after trying to call his mother.

"Why not?" Sarah asked. "I thought you planned the time."

"Yeah, but my other cousin is home, and they're having a party. . . . My sister told me it's a bad time to call."

Ken's cousins, Rob and Joe Jr., had both joined the Marines, deciding to enlist before being drafted. Rob had been wounded and had shrapnel in his lower back. It gave him pain and was enough to prevent a return to Vietnam, but he still had all his body parts. Joey's body parts had come home, but in a coffin.

"My aunt keeps wanting parties for Rob," Ken explained. "It's like she wants to party, party, party because she still has a son who's alive."

"Do they go to Joey's grave?" Sarah asked.

"Yeah. Sure. All the time. My sister said Aunt Ingrid takes flowers. Uncle Joe just goes and stands there. . . . His son the war hero and all that."

"*Was* he a hero?"

"What *is* a hero?"

Sarah couldn't answer, but the look on Roger's face told her he was trying to hold himself back from answering. Both remained silent, letting Ken go on.

"They're good people. We used to get together every Thanksgiving. . . . I remember one year when Joey and I started a food fight with mashed potatoes. . . . Boy, did we get it for that!" He laughed and shook his head. Thanksgiving dinners were always at Uncle Joe and Aunt Ingrid's house, just Dad and his brother and their wives and children. Ken and Joe Junior had always used those times to plan pranks. "So . . . no more

Beverley Dowling

Joey . . . probably no more Rob and Aunt Ingrid and Uncle Joe for me now. . . . I'm not sure about my dad. He was at Omaha and he went through a lot . . . medals . . . the whole bit. . . . No, it just wasn't a good time to call Mom."

***

"War is Hell" was written on the helmet of a young American soldier fighting in Vietnam. His face, beneath the helmet, was one of the iconic images of that war. The helmets were insufficient to protect the many who were repatriated beneath their flag, just as helmets of earlier and later wars failed to provide safety.

Civilians had no helmets, but that may have kept them closer to the realities of guns and mortar shells and bombs. All were at risk: the civilians in Vietnam, the soldiers, and the teenaged boys in their last year of school.

"Bunch of kids!" Ken screamed. He and Roger and Sarah were in the common room at his residence, watching TV coverage of the dead.

"What can we do?" Sarah asked. "There's nothing we can do, and you guys don't seem to clue in; it isn't our war!"

She was tired and wanted to just sit and macrame a long belt for a new dress. As soon as the words came out, she regretted them. The moment of silence was almost more frightening than Roger's anger when he screamed his reply.

"What do you mean by that! You know damn well what's going on! You sit there with your new belt and your flouncy blouses and flowery skirts and you say something like that! Use your head!"

He stood over her when screaming the words, and she held her hands still, not knowing what to do with the macrame string. It was Ken who changed the tone. Ken spoke softly.

"I understand. No one wants to be part of this." He looked at Roger. "But, we all are," he said, looking at Sarah.

Roger sat down beside her. "I'm sorry."

"So am I."

"There's another rally coming, " Ken mentioned. "And we have work to do."

132

By the time Roger's hand healed, the weather was warm and the days were long. Roger and Ken spent more time together while Sarah concentrated on her term papers. Roger and Sarah did take time to go to the Island and go up in Akasha. The golf courses were busy again, children were playing in parks, and the fruit farms near Niagara were in bloom. They saw nothing but beauty when in Akasha.

Akasha, as Roger called her, was always "the plane" or "it" to Sarah. For her, the plane was about a few hours of fun every so often. For him, she was a passion. All pilots are like that with their planes, just as all boaters are like that with their boats.

"She's certified for floats," Roger once told Sarah. "And they gave her a big increase in baggage space and shoulder room."

"It feels weird when you call it *she*."

"Akasha isn't just another 'it'; Akasha takes me into my best dreams."

It seemed strange that he would care about such things as float certification and cargo space, as Akasha was never used as a float plane and they didn't need baggage space. Extra shoulder room was nice to have, but Akasha was about more than mere specifications.

She took them up—above the noise and confusion—into a place of sunshine, where they could hear nothing but their own voices, in discussion about the things they chose to discuss, and the reassuring sound of the engine, keeping them safely above whatever might be below.

***

Roger and Ken became more and more passionate in their anger. They watched the news all along—the Tet Offensive, My Lai, Kent State, the bodies returning to the USA—and had met more and more young American men who were joining them in the Yorkville coffee shops and the walks down University Avenue.

Nixon said the silent majority of Americans supported the war, but they didn't see that. The Americans who joined them seemed like ordinary people, from big cities, small towns, and rural places. Their fathers had fought in World War Two, and their grandfathers in World War One. Some were able to talk to their parents regularly, even as often as on a weekly basis; others were unwelcome to call. Some called when their mothers would be at home, but their fathers would be at work.

Those who were newly arrived usually had very little money, but some were reluctant to ask that phone charges be reversed. They did not trust the authorities in their country, or even the telephone operators, to leave their families in whatever peace they could find. In the small towns and rural areas, the telephone operators knew everyone, and an operator whose son had been killed would not feel sympathy for a mother whose son was safe in Canada.

Roger and Ken started a street bank, taking donations to help the newly arrived draft dodgers and deserters. They needed food and lodging and cash for the short time period before they found jobs. They called it "Operation Switzerland." It felt very "Swiss": a banking operation in a neutral country, away from the actual war, operated by people who were not at war themselves. In joking references to Operation Switzerland, they always felt an underlying relief that it was someone else's war.

Some of the people who came north had money sent by parents or grandparents, but the ones who had nothing to draw on were helped by people who made "deposits," knowing they were really donations, and the people who drew on the money agreed to replace it when they could. Most returned that much, with interest, even though they had no obligation other than conscience.

There were times to relax, despite war and academic stress. They had music and music festivals.

"Are you going to Mariposa?" Ken asked Roger, rather than Sarah.

"Sure we will," he replied on Sarah's behalf as well as his own, without asking her.

"Let's go together," Ken continued to look only at Roger, instead of both.

"Sounds good."

"You always do that!" Sarah complained.

"Huh?" Roger didn't understand.

"You might ask me what I want instead of just choosing for me."

"You do want to go, right?" Roger didn't see his mistake. "I just thought you'd want to go."

"It isn't that. It's just . . . Oh, never mind!" She left the two of them, in her anger and their confusion.

By the weekend of the Mariposa Folk Festival, they had forgotten that episode and were as excited as anyone else on the ferry to Toronto Island. At the festival, they listened to Joni Mitchell and Joan Baez and ate hot dogs and felt ever so superior to the people in the country on the other side of the Niagara River, who were at war.

The Mariposa festivals drew huge crowds, all about the same age and all with the energy of youth. Sarah preferred long skirts, either floral print or denim, but some girls wore jeans with oversized blouses. Everyone had strings of love beads, long or short, around their necks. They were there to listen to the musical icons of their era, but there were other musicians, too. They were those who would go to the Island with guitars, balalaikas, or harmonicas, and start impromptu jam sessions on the beaches. Long hair held in place with headbands across the foreheads, like Roger's and Sarah's, was the usual style, but some people had Afros. Only the police had short hair.

The police were there to keep the peace. It was amusing to see the looks on their faces when puffs of smoke from marijuana cigarettes drifted past them. Some of the older policemen stiffened their posture when they smelled it; others fought back smiles. The younger ones looked slightly envious of the people in the crowd. There were a few arrests, but usually only if the person being arrested had done something too blatant to ignore.

Everyone knew there were plainclothes and undercover policemen in the crowd. Roger and Sarah played games with each other, trying to pick them out. Their clothes were similar to everyone else's, but if you saw someone looking around, ever so serious and paying more attention to the crowd than to the music, you would tend to blow your smoke in another direction.

***

When they were in the street car after a flight, Roger realized he had forgotten to let Sarah know what he had discussed with Ken the day before.

"Next stop—Ottawa," Roger told her. "It's big . . . people from all over moving from Parliament Hill to the US embassy. . . . We have to be part of it."

"When?"

"Next weekend. So, get your stuff ready."

She knew what to do: put only the bare essentials into the backpack, wear comfortable shoes, and take her camera and plenty of film. Roger and Ken would decide what the signs should say and assign her to paint them.

"Are we taking Akasha?"

He glared at the question, and at her. "Of course not. We're going by bus, along with everyone else."

"Where will we stay?"

"Not quite sure, but we're taking tents. People are getting things set up at that end."

"So, you're telling me you don't know?"

"Relax. There are people taking care of that part. Let them do their thing, and we'll do ours."

"After a five-hour bus ride and a hike along Wellington Street, I'll want to get some sleep. Is that going to happen?"

He didn't say anything but put his arm around her shoulders and hugged her. An answer would have been better.

"Why Ottawa? We could all just go by the American consulate here."

"The idea is to get as many people as we can going right by their embassy, and," he paused, "it's going to be later in the afternoon."

"Rush hour? That'll make a lot of people angry."

"And also get a lot more press."

"I don't know how else I can let you know that I'm getting tired of all this." His failure to acknowledge her needs and his insistence that she participate in his projects annoyed her.

Sarah wondered why she stayed with Roger at all, but she knew she would go with him. When the day came, she went to the Toronto bus terminal, as arranged, where she met Roger and Ken. There were a few people going to other places, but most were going to Ottawa. They stood and chatted or sat on their backpacks, waiting for direction.

"What do you think?" Roger asked.

"A good crowd." Ken was pleased. "The buses have been pulling out full."

"I really don't know why you guys think this is going to make any difference. I don't know why you bother."

"Use your brain!" Roger's face was red. "Ken lost his cousin. Isn't that reason enough?"

"Yes, it is. I'm sorry about your cousin. I really am. They're trying to get out of Vietnam. Nixon keeps saying it."

"Sure! Bastard Nixon!" It was the first time Ken had directed anger toward Sarah. "Tricky Dick talks about getting out. Guys like my cousin are out of the war and out of everything else. Is that what he means by 'getting out'?"

"I know. I'm really sorry about your cousin . . . and for you, it's personal, but it isn't the same for us. It isn't our war."

Roger and Ken were silently angry until Roger could no longer remain silent. "You still don't get it!"

"Take it easy, buddy. Sarah doesn't like it any more than anyone else." Ken paused, then looked at Sarah.

Sarah's pale face and slumping shoulders tempted Roger to react in a different way, but he was angry.

"Hurry up," Roger told her. "We have to get those signs down to the bus. I want them loaded in first."

"You might at least wait for the paint to dry!" Sarah replied.

"You should have finished them before this!"

"Well, for crying out loud, you're the one who kept changing your mind about what you wanted on them!"

He let her have the last word that time, which was unusual. He was preoccupied with plans for Ottawa and didn't want to bother with an argument. They carried the signs to the bus terminal and left them with friends who would load them.

"We have to make sure food is all set up," he said.

"It is. Remember?" Sarah replied.

"I want to make sure. . . . Are you coming with me?"

"Oh . . . all right." She would have preferred to sit somewhere and read.

"This is all part of what we have to do. You know that, right?"

"Yes." She had to admit that she understood. Every fine detail was needed.

It would be wrong to say "they" looked at everything the group needed for the trip. Sarah merely went along while Roger examined bags and boxes and checked off lists. When he had satisfied himself that everything was in order, he relaxed.

"Are you hungry?" Roger asked Sarah. "We should eat before we leave. Let's try that place across the street." Then he turned to Ken. "Are you coming, buddy?"

"No. You two go. I have to check a few things."

The diner near the bus terminal was busy, without being overly full. Roger insisted on a table beside the window, so he could see the activity near the buses.

"It's good to see the numbers." Roger studied the crowd.

"Isn't it what you guys expected?"

"Yes, but it's still good to see."

"What can I get you?" a waitress asked.

"Oh, we haven't looked at the menu yet," Roger answered.

"I'll come back in a few minutes."

Sarah looked at the menu while Roger ignored it, looking out the window at the gathering crowd at the terminal.

"Coming here was your idea. Are you going to eat anything?" Sarah demanded.

"Oh. Oh, yes. You order for both of us, ok?"

Sarah left the table, approached the waitress, and placed the orders while Roger continued to watch the crowd. When the waitress brought the order, Roger was still watching the terminal and had not said anything to Sarah. They ate their lunch in silence until the waitress came to take the plates.

"Coffee?" she asked.

"Yes," Sarah responded at the same time Roger answered, "No. We need to hurry."

"Why? There's time for coffee. I'll have some." Sarah smiled at the waitress, who withdrew without comment.

"I don't know whether we have enough signs."

"We do. You already know that. You checked." She was blunt.

"We need to go over there."

"I'm at least going to brush my hair!"

"Be quick about it."

"I'm going to the bathroom while I can still use a real toilet!" Her impatience was turning to anger.

"Ok. Be fast."

"No! I'm going to touch up my makeup. You can go ahead. . . . I'll be there in plenty of time." Sarah left the table.

Roger paid the waitress and left before Sarah returned. He was looking straight ahead when he stepped onto the pavement. At that moment, a middle-aged woman wearing dark clothing and an American flag on her lapel lunged at him. The man with her, who wore the same lapel pin, reached forward to stop her.

"Goddamn hippies!" the woman screamed, moving her fist toward Roger.

"Carol, no! This boy had nothing to do with it."

"Goddamn hippies think they know it all!" She was in tears. "Damn you, Gary, Bobbie's dead! Our own son! Dead!"

"Carol, honey, let's get back to the hotel."

Gary wrapped his arm around Carol while she wept on his shoulder. He kissed her on the forehead and stroked her hair. Roger moved his hand forward to comfort her. She moved back from him.

"You goddamn hippies think you know it all! You think you know better than the president! And here you are, safe in Canada! It isn't even your war, goddammit!"

Roger remained silent while she ranted. His silence was not enough. She wanted a reaction. She lunged toward him, pushing him onto the street. At that moment, there was a screech of the tires of a bus and screams from bystanders. Then silence.

Sarah was returning to the table when she saw Roger with the couple in dark clothing. She screamed and ran outside to Roger. He was unconscious, with red foam coming from his mouth.

Someone must have called an ambulance, as the siren sound started almost immediately, even though the ambulance seemed to take an hour. Someone later told Sarah it was less than five minutes. In those five minutes, she must have run to the place on the street where cars were stopped and people were screaming and Roger lay on the pavement. Perhaps she was rude, and perhaps she hurt some of the people she pushed aside.

When she bent toward him, she saw he was breathing but too much. His breathing was loud, and the sound carried the warning of liquid in his lungs. Red foam came up from his mouth with every breath. The red foam and blood from some other part of his body felt warm, even as it soaked through her blouse and skirt.

Sarah was holding Roger when the paramedics arrived. They gestured to her to step aside.

"We need space, miss," a paramedic said, reaching forward to Roger without any other explanation. At that point, she stood up and stood back.

They put tubes into his mouth and hands, bundled him in a neck brace and blankets, and strapped him to a board. When they loaded him into the ambulance, she tried to get in.

"No, only the patient. He'll be at St. Mike's."

That was good to know. She began to be hopeful and found herself thinking that if any hospital could save him, it was St. Mike's.

Everything blurred together. Sarah remembered someone pulling her away from Roger and her awareness of the need to let that happen, but she would never remember the details. A few minutes after that she became aware of Roger's blood on her clothing and her hands. It gave her images of Lady Macbeth, even though, in her case, the blood was real. She held her hands up and looked at them and didn't know what to do about the blood.

Ken came to her and hugged her. He held her back while the paramedics put Roger into the ambulance, and he arranged to have someone take her to St. Mike's.

"I have to get on that bus, Sarah. Roger would want that."

It sounded wrong, but Sarah nodded. Someone else took her to St. Mike's and bought coffee for her before they left for Ottawa. She didn't know who that person was, as they all looked the same.

By the time she arrived he was already in surgery. The waiting area for the emergency department had chairs beside the windows on the south side. She tried to remember the street name. Queen? Dundas? Adelaide? She knew all the streets and knew the area, but couldn't remember which one it was. Dundas? Adelaide? Queen?" She tried to find a way for the street name to matter, but it didn't. Even though it didn't matter, she kept trying to remember it.

The street was busy, with more activity than in the waiting room. Pedestrians on the sidewalk rushed one way or another, singly or in pairs, and unlike those in the waiting room, everyone out there appeared to have a destination. Sarah had none and felt that she was invisible to everyone else.

She approached the triage station and gave the woman behind the glass Roger's name and details.

"I saw them take him into that area. . . ."

"What is your relationship?"

"I'm his girlfriend."

"Let me have a look." The woman checked something below the level of the glass screen. "Do you have identification?"

"Yes, here." Sarah reached for her student ID card.

"Oh, I'm sorry, that isn't the name we have for next of kin."

"What is that name?"

"I can't tell you that without authority."

"But it should be me."

"These things are often oversights. Have you changed your own emergency information? Young people often forget."

Sarah left the woman without answering. She noticed a nurse leaving the area where they had taken Roger.

"Excuse me. Can you help me? My boyfriend is in there, and he'd want me to be with him."

"Sorry, but no. If you wait here I might be able to let you know more."

"When will that be?"

"That's impossible to say. Just wait."

Waiting was all Sarah could do. The changing light was imperceptible until she looked out and saw that the streetlights had come on. The pedestrians on the other side of the window moved with less urgency, and the pavement glimmered with moisture.

The same nurse came out, moving toward an exit, and then she stopped for a moment and met Sarah's eyes.

"The doctors are busy with him. I can't give details, but he is in surgery. His parents are coming. The doctors will fill them in, and they can give you details. Do you know them well?"

"I haven't met them." She realized that she didn't know what Roger's parents looked like.

When the lights outside gained greater contrast with the darkness, a middle-aged couple came into the waiting area, led by a volunteer who took them to a small room with a window. Sarah could see them saying nothing while a doctor talked to them. On Sarah's side of the glass, there was only silence

Someone came to her and said, "This is a terrible time for you. Do you know where to get coffee?"

"Yes, thank you," she said under her breath. "What are they doing now?" she asked a nurse.

"Are you related to him?" she asked.

"I'm his girlfriend."

The nurse looked at a chart.

"I'm sorry . . . I can't give any information to anyone other than next of kin."

"But he'd want me here. . . . He'd want me to know."

"Yes, I'm sure he would. The best thing to do right now is get yourself a coffee . . . or would you like me to call a chaplain? Sometimes that's all you can do."

She went for a coffee.

***

Roger's parents were still on the other side of a glass, with another doctor. The doctor came out and made notes on something at the nursing station; the nurse spoke to him. Sarah could hear nothing but saw the nurse's lips moving and her head gesturing toward her. Then the doctor went back to the parents and said something, then went to Sarah.

"This is a terrible time for you. Have you met Roger's parents?"

It was a strange introduction. It wasn't a time to say, "Pleased to meet you," or even, "Hello," so she just looked at them with her mouth partially open, wanting to say something but not knowing what to say.

"You were there, weren't you?" his mother asked, but it was more an accusation than a question. Sarah nodded. Roger's mother had mascara streaks on her cheeks, and Sarah knew that her cheeks must have been the same. His father had dry cheeks, but his eyes were red.

Roger was moved to an intensive care unit, still unconscious. His parents gave Sarah permission to see him, so she stood while they sat and the three of them listened to the whooshing of air moving through a tube, into and out of his lungs. At least, there was no red foam.

"Would you stay away for now, please?" a nurse asked Sarah. "I'm so sorry about this. . . . It's up to the next of kin and it's a very difficult time for everyone."

She took Sarah to another little room. While there, she explained what was happening. The blood on her blouse and skirt had dried to form rough patches on the fabric, the patches stiff, just as Roger's body soon would be.

"I always thought it was someone else's war."

PART THREE
SARAH'S STORY

TORONTO, 2010

It was good to have BJ near when Mum died. Tony and Lisa were grown and supportive, but they remembered her only as their grandmother. Grandmothers could never be imagined as having been young. BJ had been there for me when Dan died, just as I had been there for BJ when her husband died. Each of us had been there during the other's widowhood. Each of us had lost a husband early.

Dan was my husband. When Roger died I didn't want to love again, and thought love would never be possible. No one, not even Dan, lived up to my image of my ideal man after I lost Roger. It isn't that we didn't have a good marriage. It was solid, rather than passionate, but there is something comforting about solid relationships.

After losing Roger I thought there would be no more grief in my life, but that assumption was wrong. There were small things at first, when Dan lost his way home, or forgot appointments, but those small early signs of a larger problem could be explained away. By the time he died he was a different person. He died just a few months before Mum.

Friends told me to stay in the house for the first year, but I wanted to leave as soon as possible. Our house in the country was too big for me and my dog, and the fields and stream no longer gave me pleasure. The garden gave comfort, but the house was overwhelming.

***

BJ spent the day before my mum's funeral with me and pointed out that we both needed to have our hair done. After the hair appointment, we had lunch and walked through a mall.

"This sounds crazy, but I want to do my Christmas shopping early, in bits and pieces." I needed reminders of happiness.

"Right you are, Sarah. It's so much better." BJ understood.

"So, let's go shopping."

"Why not?"

I bought mechanical things Tony would like and Lisa's perfume before moving on. I saw a collection of linens with lavender embroidery.

"Oh, Mum would love these! I'll pick them up for her!"

"No, of course not." BJ gave me a gentle smile and said nothing.

There was nothing more to do about the funeral, but I was left with the strange feeling of needing to be busy. Others helped, but it felt important to be the main organizer. Lisa and Tony had called friends and family, and BJ had arranged the catering. Lisa helped sort old photographs, unaware of who most of the people in the older ones were.

The church could seat two hundred and fifty people comfortably. The three hundred who attended the funeral were there as much for me as for Mum, and that thought gave comfort, which made me feel guilty, as the event was not about me. It was also comforting that BJ was there and Ken had come from Washington. BJ and I had shared lives. Ken was Roger's old friend, but he and Dan had become close. He was more a friend for Dan than me, even though I had known him so much longer, so I appreciated his kindness in coming to Mum's funeral.

The service was traditional, and the only thing that seemed odd was the priest's comment that, "Edith had a long life and, by all appearances, a happy one." Long was correct, but I wondered about the word "happy." Born into a war, growing up through a depression and social upheaval, living through another war, and losing the man she loved to the Gestapo were all parts of her life. On the other hand, the priest was right, as there was always a spirit of happiness. She had chosen to be happy.

A few of the people who shook my hand after the funeral noticed my bracelet. BJ remembered that it was Mum's.

"It's nice to see you wearing your mother's bracelet."

"Yes, it's a special one."

"It's pretty. When did she get it?"
"A man gave it to her, but that's all I know. There's an inscription."
"Let me see." BJ reached over to touch it.
"Ok." I showed the bracelet to her without removing it.
"I can't make out the whole thing. Is that an H?"
"I think so."

The engraved inscription was worn and almost indecipherable. It showed an H and an E on the back of the central oval, and delicate painting on the others. There was a sleigh with a reindeer on the central one, and tiny flowers on the others.

BJ stayed close after the service, while Tony and Lisa walked from table to table, chatting with friends and family they saw only at weddings and funerals. They asked each other which were the friends and which were the family, as years change looks.

"Let's get coffee," BJ suggested.
"Mum always preferred tea."
"Ok. Tea, then. This is her party. I'll get it."

BJ gestured to Tony and Lisa. "You two stay with your mum while I get tea."

While BJ went for the tea, I showed Tony and Lisa photos of their grandmother. They saw themselves and their parents at the beach, and at fall fairs and family reunions. They saw their Nana in the garden and at picnics in the park. They saw her in groups with the Canadian aunts and uncles, and recognized everyone in most of the pictures. It was easy to identify the Canadian relatives, but there were other pictures that had been kept in a dresser drawer rather than in albums which could be pulled out easily.

There she was, as a young woman in a flapper hairstyle, as one of a group of women in military uniform, some with children who were her siblings, some with Uncle Peter, in army uniform, and some with a tall handsome man in RAF uniform. Some showed her with the same man, standing on a bridge over the pond in St. James' Park. Others showed her and the same man feeding pigeons.

It was a surprise to find a picture of Mum and myself with Roger. I remembered Bruni taking that picture, all those years ago. That was another era, and I didn't realize that she had kept that picture.

BJ approached, tea in hand.

"Here you go. Are you going to sit or carry it?"

"Let's sit. Have you seen these?"

"No. Old photos are always interesting."

"This one is her sister, Pat."

"You call her 'Pat' instead of 'Aunt Pat'?"

"She says she won't be called 'Aunt' by anyone as old as I am. Allow her that small bit of vanity. She is closer in age to me than to Mum, so it isn't all that strange."

"She was a cute kid."

"And now she's a beautiful woman."

"She was gorgeous."

"Yes. Lisa looks a lot like her."

"It's impossible to replace your mother," BJ spoke softly, drifting into her own memories. "When my mom died, I couldn't do anything but mope around. You were a great help to me."

"And you are to me, but now I'm losing you, too." I felt grateful for BJ's presence, but resentful of her for her plans to move.

"It's just a move. I'm not even leaving the country, so I'll be back to visit."

"It won't be the same."

"Of course not. It will be different, but it can still be good." BJ took my hand.

"I don't know how."

"You can be exasperating. Let go." At that point, she pulled her hand back and shook her head.

"Right. Let's just plan a few good things before you leave." I relented, feeling slightly guilty about my selfishness in wanting to keep her nearby.

"That's the spirit!"

BJ wondered about the man who approached. She had heard him chatting and recognized an American accent.

"Have you two met?" I asked.

"No. I'm BJ." She held out her right hand, using the left to stroke hair behind her ear. "Just a friend."

"Ken Becker, another friend, but you'll never get me to say 'just' about friends." He smiled while shaking her hand.

"I stand corrected. Wait a minute . . . you were Dan's friend from the States. He told everyone about the fishing trips."

"They were good times. I wasn't just Dan's friend, though. Sarah and I go back a long way." He smiled at me while saying it. "Way before she met Dan."

Tony and Lisa joined them, and Tony spoke up. "Those fishing trips were great. Some of my best memories."

"I'm glad you remember them. You were pretty young." Ken smiled at Tony.

"Oh, I remember! And shore lunches. You always caught the best fish, and then you guys started fighting about hockey and baseball."

"I wouldn't call it fighting." Ken laughed. "It was just friendly national rivalry. He always thought hockey is better than baseball."

"He was right!"

"Not to me! I love baseball." Ken turned back to me. "So, how are you doing?"

"Getting on."

"It's tough when you don't have Dan here. Heck, it's tough for me; I miss him, too. You've been through this before, haven't you?"

"So, how long are you going to be around?" BJ asked Ken, changing the topic and giving him her warmest smile while tilting her head to match the angle of his.

"Not sure. I have a few things to do." He hesitated before turning to me. "So, what are you going to do with your mom's ashes?"

"I'm not sure. I haven't thought that far ahead."

Tony and Lisa looked at each other before Tony responded, "Why not? You knew she was dying."

"It isn't that simple," Lisa answered. "Give it a bit of time."

"Why?" he persisted.

BJ decided to change the topic. "Don't you two want food?"

When Tony and Lisa went to the sandwich table, Ken and BJ stayed with me.

"If there's anything you need . . ." Ken began to speak but stopped himself. "She seems like a good friend." Ken gestured toward BJ when she went for more tea.

"Yes, but I'm losing her, too. She's moving west."

"Far west?"

"All the way."

"So, what are you going to do?"

"What do you mean? There isn't much I can do to stop her."

"I don't mean that. Why not be happy for her? Why not give her a going away party?"

"Maybe." I resented BJ's plan. "I'll think about it."

"Just do it. You know you will. Will you invite me?" He seemed eager, and I suspected BJ's warm smile had had the effect she intended.

"If you want to come all this way."

He left me feeling that I had made a commitment to have a party, a commitment made on the day of my mother's funeral.

**

After the funeral and the reception, there was nothing to do. BJ offered to come back to my house, but being alone with Angel, my lovely old dog, was best and wandering in the garden seemed essential. Angel chased geese and rolled happily in the excrement while I sniffed flowers. The peonies were hinting at bud; the ones closest to bloom made me think of the fragrance my mother always enjoyed; I remembered her saying she could never be without flowers. The peony was an old one and popular in England. Roses and mint and lavender would come out later, and combine to give a fresh fragrance that seemed to be labelled "Edith."

Clipping a few late lilacs for the house was almost automatic, so the freshness of garden flowers would contrast with the dying smell of funeral arrangements. The chatter of birds and the rustle of leaves were interrupted by another sound, impossible to ignore. A Cessna, like Akasha, approached the area. I had stopped thinking of her as

"Roger's plane" or "it" and had memories of Akasha. The pilot took it in circles and wide arcs, sometimes diving, sometimes soaring, sometimes banking to left or right. It was easy to identify it as a training plane from the nearby flight school.

The pilot trainee would be concerned about perfecting movements, but the view would be impossible to ignore. It would include fields with cattle, people playing golf, and children in playgrounds. There would be both countryside below and the city in the distance. To the north, there were hills and woods, and to the south, Lake Ontario. With a bit more altitude, the pilot would see Niagara Falls and have a view of another country.

The grass was growing almost as fast as the weeds in the flowerbeds, and I had to deal with both. I had mown part of the lawn a few days earlier, but it looked just as shaggy as before that mowing.

The garden, which had given such joy, had become overwhelming. It was wonderful in its day. The first time someone asked to feature it on a garden tour I was flattered and agreed immediately. It was the least "perfect" garden on the tour, but there was an easy solution to that problem; BJ came up to help host the tour. We passed trays of white wine and lemonade. Some people chose the lemonade. Despite its lack of perfection, it was one of the most popular gardens on the tour. That was all in the past, and we all have to create a future. Angel and I had to move on.

The late lilacs competed in fragrance with the mock orange. The catkins were long gone, but the branches of pussy willow had soft green leaves. I collected flowers and stems and carried them into the kitchen. While cutting the stems, I clicked on the radio. That was a mistake, as the news distracted me from the joy of flowers.

NORAD was conducting military flight exercises over the area in preparation for G-8 and G-20 meetings. People living in and around Toronto might be "buzzed" by military jets flying at low altitudes. They were flying from the Island airport. Along with a luxury airline, the Island was home to more military flights.

The next news clip was about a volcano in Iceland, spewing ash, with winds blowing it into patterns no one would have predicted.

The ash cloud was affecting air traffic as far south as Spain, causing mass confusion.

It wasn't just a matter of flights into and out of two countries with closed airports. People flying from Cairo to London or from New York to Shannon were affected. American tourists exploring their Irish roots couldn't get home, nor could the English priests who were meeting colleagues in Rome. A volcano with an unpronounceable name, in a distant country, disrupted the entire world.

The news about the Icelandic ash cloud reminded me that I had to deal with other ashes. Tony was right; it would have been better to have a plan before the death rather than look for one after. On the other hand, planning the disposal of the remains of a human being seemed to make the loss come earlier. There was no right way to approach the physical reality.

Whether my way was right or wrong, Ken had asked a question that needed an answer. Dad was buried in the local cemetery, so that seemed the best place. It wasn't quite that simple, though. Mum's life was about much more and taking some part of the ashes back to England seemed right. Everyone who attended the funeral knew she was English, but very few knew any more than that about the time before she came to Canada. Most were surprised when they saw photos of the woman they thought they had known wearing military uniform.

The Canadian family knew most of the people in the pictures taken after World War Two, even though those photos were cracked and fading. "Oh, doesn't she look nice in this one" or "Sarah was just a baby then" and the occasional "Is that Aunt Elsie?"

The photos taken in England were mysterious, so they attracted more attention. The back of each photo had a note, in pencil, in elegant italic script: "Jimmy and his cricket bat," "Anne and Dad, by the Anderson shelter," "Peter, day he signed up," "Pat in marrow patch," "with Harald St. James' Park."

"So, who's that good looking guy?" Aunt Peggy asked.

"Oh, he was an old flame."

"Lucky Edie! I'll bet there's a story about that one!"

The photos did tell a story, but it was a story without an ending.

"Yes, but she never told me the details."

"Was he killed in action?"

"I don't know all the details, and the details don't really matter. Mum never said much, but she did say something about him being a spy, or working with spies, and that made his work more dangerous. She was always really angry at any mention of the Gestapo. I'm sure there's a connection."

"He's in uniform."

"Yes, but you can see everything from the air. I suppose a pilot could get a lot of information."

"I wish I had asked her more questions."

"She wouldn't have answered."

Tony brought Amber to the house the next day. Amber, his dog, was a lively boxer puppy, unaware of bad things and, therefore, without fear.

"Hi, Mum, got anything to eat?"

"Look in the fridge. There are lots of leftovers." I was in no mood to cook for him and didn't care whether he found food or not.

"Won't they be yucky by now?"

"Have a look. You can pick and choose for yourself."

He found sandwiches that were still edible and gave a few to Amber. She gulped them down and begged for more.

"You should keep her on dog food."

"She's ok. She'll eat whatever I give her, but she likes this stuff better than dog food."

"We need to clear out the house. You should go through your room."

"I did that as soon as you said you're moving. I don't know why it's taking you so long. All you have to do is pitch out your junk, and most of it is junk."

"Don't you feel sentimental about anything?" I asked. His coldness was annoying.

"Sure, but I've already taken those things. You have to get at it." He ignored my frown and remained calm.

Tony and Amber left the house in a mess. Bits of torn paper were all over the floor of the entrance room, bearing witness to the presence of a lively little dog, shredded and still wet with her saliva. She was small for the breed and would almost be described as "dainty" if she were not so active. She was ten years younger than Angel, who was gentle and wise.

During the peaceful moments after Tony and Amber left, Angel stood at the door, hinting that she wanted to go outside, so the two of us took a slow walk across the lawn. Birds were singing. They flew from branch to branch of the old catalpa trees that were ready to fall to their fate the next time a strong wind blew. For then, there was only a breeze. The catalpas remain, and birds continue to nest in them.

***

Returning to work the following Monday was strange. I was on a scholarship selection team, and we had to decide which applicants should win. After making the priority list, we broke for lunch. Kelly and Julian, my colleagues on the selection committee, were hungry and tired. Talk turned to their own lives: the latest baseball scores, Kelly's investigation into daycare, and plans for the summer.

"For me, the next few months will be about my mum," I said.

They looked puzzled, knowing she was dead.

"I have to get the main urn interred with my dad, but a small container has to go to England." I explained.

"So, you're going on a holiday?" Julian asked.

"If you want to call it that."

"When do you leave?" Kelly wondered.

"Not sure, but July looks right for my family. My only concern is how to get there."

"Well, that's obvious; you book a flight." Julian had the simple answer.

"Maybe not so obvious; that volcano may blow again and I don't want to be stranded."

"HAH!" Julian laughed. "Stranded in Europe? Staying with relatives? *Biiiiig* problem!"

"No, really, it could be bad."

"So, how will you go?" Kelly wondered.

"Surface."

"Ah! A cruise!" "Yes, boat . . ." "I'd love a cruise. . . ."—they talked over each other, the level of excitement rising as each considered cruise travel.

"Not exactly."

"Huh?"

"I want something special. I was thinking of going by freighter." I explained, thinking it sounded exciting.

There was dead silence.

***

On the way home, I went to the mall, where I saw Ellen, the funeral director who had handled things for Mum. It was the first time I had seen her in anything other than a black suit and hair pulled back in a low bun; she was almost unrecognizable in jeans and a T-shirt, with her hair at her shoulders. She gave me a generous smile.

"Hi, I've been thinking about you. Have you decided what to do with your mom's ashes? No rush, but I was just wondering."

"I'm not sure. Could I take a small container of them to England?" Whether or not I could travel by freighter, I had to deal with the ashes.

"No problem. People carry ashes all the time. When you know what you want to do, just come in and I'll get everything ready."

I saw her the next day. She was in her usual uniform of black suit, with hair pulled back, and looked much older than she did in the jeans.

"Come in," she welcomed me in her casual, friendly way. "The rules are easy to follow. You need a death certificate and a cremation certificate, and we have those for you. You have to carry the ashes in a hermetically sealed container."

"What on earth is that?"

"It's this." She picked up a plastic film canister. "It's exactly what you need, and I've already put the ashes in."

"How do I open it?"

"Like this." She smiled and popped the top of the container. A small puff of grey ash moved up, a small cloud of my mother's molecules blending into the air. "That's it. Now you just have to arrange your flight."

It was so simple, and so easy.

***

Viduity. What a harsh word. It means "widowhood" or "the state of being a widow." I had never heard it before entering my own viduity, searching the Internet for sites about widowhood.

One site gave a link to an old court case involving a woman who was given the use of her husband's lands during her "chaste viduity." When her baby was born too long after her husband's death, the issue was her "chastity." She lost her husband, then her reputation, and then her livelihood. Then she died, so it all became moot. Whether moot or not, the court case was reported and her name was placed before the public as "unchaste." I wondered about how and by whom her child was conceived. Was she betrayed by a lover? Raped by her husband's heir? Who would ever have known other than the widow herself and the anonymous man?

Despite constant awareness of my own viduity, there was reminder after reminder that life goes on. Ozzie and Harriet came back. Ozzie and Harriet are the Canada Geese who use the pond every year. They walked across the lawn with newly hatched goslings. They couldn't be the same Ozzie and Harriet who were there years earlier, but they did seem to know me. Perhaps they were descendants of the first Ozzie and the first Harriet. Whether or not, they were there with a new generation.

Tony kept calling, checking in on me. He understood that Dan's slow decline made me a widow long before, and it had just become official. Even so, the change in marital status when filling out forms seemed strange.

Dan was a packrat, so there were things in my house that should have been thrown away years earlier. My decision to move forced me to go through the details of my life. Most of the details were of no practical use, even though some small bits of paper brought back memories of better times. The waste disposal people only allowed four bags of garbage per household every two weeks, along with unlimited recycling and compost. I usually created less than half a bag of garbage for each pickup day, but routinely put out four bags. Bag tags allowed me to put out extras. There were weeks when I put out twenty bags of garbage, along with extra blue bins filled with things to be recycled.

The charities did well, too. I went through the house each day, putting garbage into black bags and donations to charities into orange ones. I dragged the black bags to a shed near the road, making it easier to put them out on pickup day, and put the orange ones into the back seat of the car. Stopping at a thrift store donation point became part of my daily routine. All the possessions were excess, to be disposed of. It seemed so strange to see them as "excess" or "disposable"; these were things we had collected over the course of our lives. Some went back to other lives. There were two little copper dishes that Mum had given me, passed down from her own mother. They were of no value, other than in my own mind, but parting with them seemed wrong.

Lisa sorted through her old bedroom. Getting the house ready to sell meant repainting rooms. Tony's was the colour of a Halloween pumpkin and Lisa's bright fuchsia. The painter was ready to start, so the rooms had to be emptied.

Lisa brought out her supply of black and orange bags when facing decisions. She had a question about nearly every item.

"Mum, Nana gave me these a long time ago and I've never worn them, but, well, you know . . . Nana." Lisa obviously understood the importance of things connected with her nana, whether or not those things were of other value. I agreed with her, but didn't say so.

She held out a small box containing a string of faux pearls with a rather large faux opal pendant, a brooch in the shape of a centipede with sparkles on its back, and a brooch in the shape of a large butterfly with blue and aqua glittery beads.

"I mean . . . this would be ok," she held up the faux pearls, "if it didn't have this," she pointed to the faux opal. "I might even wear it."

When I examined the necklace, I noticed the clasp at the base of the faux opal. It was easily opened, leaving the pearls in attractive simplicity.

"Actually, that butterfly isn't all that bad," I pointed out. "I have a plain navy-blue dress; I could wear it."

"This little bug isn't all that terrible," Lisa held up the centipede.

"Right. Leave it with me. Maybe one of us will use these some day."

***

Ozzie and Harriet flew on, whether or not they were the first Ozzie and the first Harriet. Those geese were oblivious to Icelandic volcanoes, and to petty problems. They walked their goslings across the lawn in optimism. Life is new. Life is fresh. Life is about the future.

There was news from Afghanistan, and the ongoing war there. Another Canadian soldier was killed by a roadside bomb. The news reported that he was twenty-four years old and enjoyed fishing, camping, and the outdoors. That could have been a description of Tony. He was with others. Why was there no news about the others? No information was given. It seemed silly to grieve a single soldier, when there must have been other deaths every day. The death of a Canadian is front page news in Canada, but what about all the others? They are reported but not to the same extent. Are they not just as dead?

Lilac time faded to peony time. The range from white to light pink to deep pink to red was more striking in the early evening, when the red of peonies disappeared and the white remained bright. I had accepted the advice given by Ken, and he had accepted my invitation to BJ's party.

It was a lovely day for a party. The house was in order, with lots of peonies, fresh from the garden, welcoming with fragrance. Some were red and some were white, but most were in various shades of pink, BJ's favourite colour. There were two big boxes, wrapped in pink, matching the pink napkins and ribbons. It was hard to know what to give someone who had just decluttered her entire house, but a camera to email photos to old friends and a calling card case with cards to use when meeting new ones seemed right. BJ had divested herself of her possessions, but friends felt driven to give her new possessions.

Most of the day was spent in preparation for the party, but while shopping for wine and balloons, I dropped in at a travel agency. The Icelandic volcano had not been in the news lately, and Mum's ashes had to get to England.

"These are good flights," the agent insisted, "but if you really enjoy sea travel, you could do it easily. The cruises are—"

"I'm not keen on cruises."

"If you travel by sea, it's a cruise. What else?"

"A freighter."

"Ah, yes, that is possible, but it isn't as easy as you might think." She gave me a patronizing smile. "A cruise is more realistic."

Freighter was still my first choice, but it was more complicated than it sounded. Freighters do not plan their routes in accordance with the wishes of passengers. There was no freighter going directly from Montreal or Halifax to Southampton. It was possible to go to London by freighter by way of Havana, Antwerp, and Liverpool or by way of South Carolina and Naples, Italy, but none seemed like a feasible plan. The travel agent suggested various options, all by air. It seemed the world relied on air travel for everything.

"On this one, you leave at 9:35 in the evening and get there . . ." The agent turned the conversation back to flights and talked about schedules, and it sounded as though the scheduling was very convenient. I would leave Pearson International at a civilized time, slightly after Toronto's notorious evening rush hour, and arrive in London at a time convenient for my Aunt Pat and her husband, David, just after their notorious morning rush hour. Even so, freighter was still my first choice.

Whenever I mentioned travel by freighter to someone, they laughed. The only exception was Lisa. She understood that neither a flight nor a cruise could offer the same kind of adventure. Taking Mum's ashes across the Atlantic was something that could be done only once, so doing something else "once" was an attractive possibility.

***

BJ's party went on into the night, with the noise level rising throughout the evening. It began quietly, with Prahma and Alak and Joan, who were all rather shy, arriving at the same time. The four of us sat, trying to think of things to say, while looking out toward the road, hoping other people would arrive.

They did arrive, and the noise level kept rising as they kept coming.

Remnants of the party were left to be put away the next day. The house was filled with happy litter: empty wine and beer bottles, leftover food to wrap in foil for Tony's snacks and lunches, scrunched napkins and paper plates, crumbs of food on the floor.

Tony came to help and let Amber have her freedom. She was excited about the changes in the house. She sniffed the floor, searching for crumbs of food. Angel, in her old age, simply stayed on her bed, enjoying the soft treats offered to her.

My aunt called that morning and talked about plans for the summer. She and David had new plans for bridge lessons, and both were excited about their cruises and about the visit. We joked a bit about the benefits of cruises, and the lack of worry about ash clouds from distant volcanoes.

Their cruise to the Canary Islands went well. My visit could be between their trip to Norway and North Cape and the Baltic Cities cruise. If that didn't work, it could be between the Baltic and the Western Mediterranean. Assuming all was well, we planned for July.

Aunt Pat had a few ideas about trips into London: perhaps a ride on the Thames, a visit to Sissinghurst, a tour of Hever Castle. Yes, all that sounded wonderful. They were emphatic about seeing Eastbourne.

"Yes, we have to go down to the sea," she said. "It's so lovely, and the view from Beachy Head is wonderful."

She asked about Mum's ashes.

"I'm not completely sure where to scatter them. Mum was so much a Londoner that somewhere in London seems right."

"I suppose we could take a ride on the Thames and sprinkle them into the water."

"Yes, but where?"

"Well, near Westminster maybe, or Tower Bridge. Tower Bridge is iconic. No other view says London as clearly as Tower Bridge."

"Actually, thinking of Westminster," I answered. "I know you mean into the water beside the Houses of Parliament, but what about the Abbey? Don't you think she deserves the Abbey?"

She burst out laughing. "You can't just go in and bury her in the Abbey! You have to get permission for things like that!"

"We could do it secretly."

"No!" She coughed out the word, while laughing.

"The only problem is I wouldn't want to sprinkle them where they could be vac'ed. It wouldn't be nice to think of Mum getting vac'ed up."

"So, it can't be the Abbey, can it?"

"Well, there is that patch of grass in the cloister. Surely they don't vac grass."

"Have you thought of Beachy Head?"

"What?"

"Beachy Head. Just above Eastbourne." She had returned to being serious. "The RAF flew over Beachy Head during the war and they had special radio towers. It was important."

The chalk cliffs extend along the southeast coast of England. Vera Lynn sang about bluebirds over the white cliffs of Dover, but the cliffs are far more extensive than the area around Dover. Beachy Head, with its high cliff, overlooks Eastbourne.

That area had been part of the defence system for hundreds of years. In 1588, beacons were erected along the cliffs, including one at Beachy Head. They were covered with pitch, which could signal with fire by night or smoke by day. A signal from the beacons was intended to warn the country of imminent invasion. The Spanish Armada failed its attempt.

Over the centuries various battles were fought at Beachy Head, so the head, the cliff, and the seacoast below were bloodied. Then, it became a place for local people to remember the RAF planes flying over. Even then, despite the war, it was beautiful.

***

"This is the anniversary of the 1980 eruption of Mount St. Helens." I called BJ after seeing the news item. "The article said there were two serious earthquakes minutes before the explosion"

"You have to stop watching the news," BJ responded. "You're talking about history, and it's over."

"That mountain sent ash sixty thousand feet into the air and wind blew it for hundreds of miles."

"It's history, not news."

"It was horrible. The ash cloud made streetlights go on during the day."

"So what? It's over."

"You don't understand."

"Oh, yes, I do."

"How can I get to England while that volcano in Iceland might keep going?"

"Oh, don't be silly. Just book the flight."

***

My lawyer wanted to see me about Dan's estate. There were papers to sign.

"Oh, I'm sorry," the receptionist apologized. "Ralph was called to court on an emergency. I tried to call you, but you must have already left. I tried your cell."

"It's not your fault. I forgot to charge it. Can I sign the papers?"

"He'll want to go over everything with you. I'm sorry."

It was annoying but gave me a free day. Ralph's office was near the ferry docks, and a visit to the Island seemed a good way to make the best of the day.

The ferries to Toronto Island had seen long service. They were refinishing woodwork on the oldest; it was celebrating one hundred years of service and deserved a centennial refurbishing. Others were more recent, but all had an aura of a bygone time. They were in use at a time when ferry passengers could watch RAF trainees from Little Norway practise their skills, and they were in use when Roger flew over the same harbour and the same islands.

The ferry moved out slowly. I looked back to the city, the skyline of luxury hotels and luxury condos and luxury boats and luxury planes, now dominated by the CN Tower. The Island was lovely at any time of year, but in spring, when paint was fresh and the decks were clean, it had the freshness of new beginnings.

I was still thinking about new beginnings when a crew member smiled at me and said, "Pretty from here, isn't it?"

"It is. I've always enjoyed this view. It's so peaceful."

"Yes. We need views like this," he paused and became sad and serious, "Have you heard any more about those soldiers?"

"What soldiers?"

"Afghanistan again. Five Americans, one Canadian, and twelve Afghan civilians."

"Oh, no. Killed?"

"A suicide bomber."

"It just doesn't stop, does it?"

"No," He paused again, and looked back toward the western end of the Island. "You see the airport?"

"Of course. Look at all the planes."

"Fancy planes now, but it was a base in World War Two."

"Oh, yes, I know about Little Norway."

He became animated. "Oh, yeah! Norwegian guys trained there. They were good!"

There are stories of the attractive young men, serious and mature beyond their years, flying from the Island, circling the harbour and the city, and manoeuvring their planes in strange patterns.

One was killed in a collision with the Sam McBride, the ferry Roger and I so often took to the Island. The trainee flew too low and too fast. His plane made contact with the wheelhouse. His trainer, who was beside him, escaped from the plane, but the pilot went into the water. He died here, in a friendly but foreign land.

The small craft flying from the same airport since then have been pleasure planes. I saw one that looked like a Cessna 172 and made me think of Roger, with his long hair and his wire-framed glasses and his serious face, sitting in Akasha talking about Vietnam or rainbows or sunlight on the waves while we circled the Island and the harbour and the city.

He would fly out over the south side of the Island, where the sand dunes were constantly shifting, and look out over the lake to another country. That country was at war, and ours was not. We were aware of it and protested against it, but to me it was always someone else's war until, suddenly, it wasn't.

The sand dunes on the south side of the longest island looked permanent, but I knew the permanence was an illusion. It was once a peninsula and became an island only when a storm tore away land at the east end. The sand dunes changed their shape and their size, despite human effort to stabilize them. The old lighthouse, which used to be at the water's edge and led mariners to safety, was now away from the water and almost hidden by vegetation. The CN Tower now provided the navigation point.

Small planes, Cessnas, circled the Island, the pilots taking them out over the lake. There's a beach there where clothing is optional, and the pilots would often take that route. When Roger flew alone, he would sometimes fly over BJ's house in the country, over the lawn where she and I used to sunbath naked.

The Toronto Island Park is part of the city in legal theory, but it felt like another place evocative of another time. The air felt cooler and the sounds were of birds and waves lapping at the sand dunes and beaches. There were no smells of cars or city dust, but of the trees and grass and the lake. This was where Roger and I would come for strolls and picnics after flying.

Returning to the city, I stood at the bow of the ferry and watched the tall buildings become overwhelming as the boat got closer to the dock. The cool wind made my eyes water, and tears fell, even though I was not really crying.

***

Going into the garden was the best thing to do on a lovely day, with weather just warm enough and just cool enough to be outside. I decided to burn more of the things that had to be burned. I arranged the fire and stirred it into flames, then let it settle down to a slow but steady burn. After that, I looked for things the scrap metal dealer might want. As I pulled out the poles for an old tent, I heard a motor above. It was another pleasure plane. The pilot was having fun, dipping the wings before flying away.

Did the pilot know me? Why would a stranger dip a wing? Or is it perfectly all right to dip a wing to a stranger in much the same way people would incline their heads and men would tip their hats during the time when Mum walked along promenades by the sea?

Dust from gathered refuse entered my mouth and caused me to gag. The only thing to do was go inside to rinse my mouth and drink fresh water.

The radio announced another homecoming, so there would be people on the bridges the next day, to see another convoy on the Highway of Heroes, for another Canadian soldier coming home beneath the flag. The planes would arrive at the Canadian Forces Base at Trenton, which was unknown to most of the country before the Afghan war. There would be ramp ceremonies, usually at Kandahar, and then the flag covered casket would travel, perhaps by way of Germany, to a Canadian Forces base near a small Ontario town that should be better known as a destination for sports fishermen.

At CFB Trenton, the casket would be met by the family, of course, and by various dignitaries. The governor general would almost certainly be there, and perhaps the prime minister or the minister of defense. From there, it would travel along the Highway of Heroes, usually known as the 401, to the coroner's office in Toronto for the necessary examination and legal formalities.

The necessary examination and the legal formalities must take place, but the better things happened on the bridges. On every overpass from CFB Trenton to Toronto, hundreds of people would stand, holding small or large Canadian flags. The people on the bridges arrived early and waited patiently for the cortege.

The groups on the bridges were not "official"; they were ordinary people of no specific rank or position, taking a bit of time from the routines of their day to stand on the bridges to support a grieving family and honour a fallen soldier. The governor general and the political leaders were duty bound to be present at CFB Trenton, but the anonymous people on the bridges stood for other reasons.

When I returned to the garden, I saw more planes, all small and probably all from the flight school. They made me fantasize about flying, soaring up through the clouds. The fantasy reminded me of Roger and of Akasha dancing upward toward the changing patterns of clouds. The clouds made images, grey on grey, of lions and fish and whales and boats and airplanes, all reminding me of Roger. When we flew, we were above everything else in so many ways—above the Island, above the lake, above Little Norway and Camp X, where spies were trained. When we flew, we could circle and dive and dip the wings. We were in the air, carried by the wind and his whims.

We could fly over Queen's Park, where legislators were making laws, and over courthouses, where those laws would be interpreted. From the air, we could ignore the gritty details of what might be happening inside those buildings and focus on the architecture and its loveliness.

We saw the beauty of the city, even in the fine details of ugliness. A prostitute on Jarvis Street might be chatting with an old panhandler and give him a few coins. A copper walking the beat on Dovercourt Road and Bloor Street might stop to chat with a storekeeper. Even in the ugly places, there was beauty when we flew above it.

My daydreaming was interrupted by smoke. The smoke from burning rubbish was too much for my throat and lungs. I showered and washed my hair and put my clothes into the washing machine, but nothing could take the taste of smoke from my mouth or the pain of it from my lungs. I tried brushing my teeth and drinking tea, then plain water and lemon juice.

In fresh clothing, with the doors and windows tightly closed, I monitored the smoke from within the house. It was a good day to have a fire, with enough of a breeze to keep the fire alive, but not so strong a wind that flames would spread across the lawn. The smoke usually rose up in a wide pillar, but occasionally the breeze changed, sending smoke swirling in another direction. Sometimes, there seemed to be a small whirlwind around the dying fire.

Things from Dan's office rose in smoke, drifting up and out over the area. There were old photos of our trip to Pompeii. Yes, there was the tour group, entering a room with casts in glass cases. The casts looked like bodies, but the bodies have long since decayed. The casts were made from the cavities left in the solidified ash after the bodies had decomposed. The casts show the bodies as they were at the moment of being encased by falling ash. They hold their arms over their heads, in a futile attempt at self-protection. When the tour group saw the casts the reaction was a unison of "ahhh," in compassion for those strangers who died so long ago, smothered by ashes.

While looking out the kitchen window, watching smoke, I clicked on the radio, only to hear more news of death in a distant war. There was an ad for a jewellery store in Yorkville, a reminder of luxury encouraging us to forget bad things and enjoy trinkets. I turned off the radio to avoid the ad and more news of war.

Dan left a mess. Decluttering takes far more time and energy than anyone else can realize and it goes on for far too long. Burning rubbish became a daily task. Rubber gloves were essential, and the smell of smoke permeated the house even with the doors and window tightly shut.

Planes continued to fly over. On a lovely day for flying some of them dipped their wings. Most were probably pleasure craft, but with some of them commercial on a small scale.

A pilot came to us once, with aerial photos of our house. He had taken them from various angles. He wanted us to buy them, for what seemed to be an exorbitant price. For an even more exorbitant price, he would have them framed and dated and have a plaque on the frame engraved with our names.

Those photos showed the fire pit, the gardens, a fallen branch that I had not noticed, and even the garden tools left on a bench. I had forgotten where I had left my rose pruner before he showed us the photographs. Dan was intrigued, and thought it might be nice to have the pictures. I found it intrusive. We thanked the pilot for showing us the photos and told him to have a good day.

***

Perfect weather arrived for Victoria Day. The entire weekend was warm and sunny, not completely still, but not too breezy. It was just right for fireworks. BJ invited me to her house for dinner, to have steak and salad, and then look for a fireworks display. The invitation was last minute, so I had to go empty handed, as the stores were closed and I didn't have any wine.

I stubbed my toe on a box in her front room. It was almost inevitable, as boxes took up most of the space.

"I thought you decluttered." The stubbed toe and her mess were annoying. "Why do you still have so much?"

"It's mostly clothes and my special books. I can't get rid of those."

"So, you really are going?"

"I have to move on. My friends are here, but I want to be near my family. Life goes on, and I have to go with it." She stopped talking for a moment before looking at me directly and asking, "Are you ok?"

"My toe hurts."

"Hah! On another topic, can you set up another way for me to see that Ken guy?"

"No point in that. He lives in the States and spends a lot of time in Berlin."

"Berlin? Why?"

"Family. Some old lady."

"If he gives up the old lady, I'd be willing to offer a younger one."

With picnics in the parks, face painting for children, and perhaps pony rides, Victoria Day marks the beginning of the summer. The amusement parks would open, and were always busy; Centreville would be packed with people on Victoria Day.

Centreville is on Toronto Island. For a few dollars, you can buy a wristband, allowing you to spend an entire day going on as many rides as you want. It has a small Ferris wheel, an old-fashioned carousel, a flume ride, a little train, bumper cars, swan boats, a roller coaster, and a sky car that takes you over the petting zoo — my favourites, but there are others. After or between rides you can eat hot dogs or ice cream cones or cotton candy or relax with a glass of wine in the café overlooking the ponds.

The papers that weekend showed pictures of people enjoying Wasaga Beach, a long stretch of fine white sand within easy driving distance. Mum and Dad always took us there for our summer holidays.

The news also revealed other things. Over the weekend, there were major Taliban attacks in both Kabul and Kandahar. There was continuing unrest in Thailand. The uprising there was crushed, but the people were still defiant. There would be more bloodshed. Sanctions were imposed on North Korea because of the sinking of a South Korean ship. Wars continued, with threats of other wars, and seemingly small diplomatic incidents.

There was more news from Afghanistan. It was a day to go to beaches and amusement parks, but there would be another ramp ceremony and then another soldier brought home and driven along the Highway of Heroes. That one was twenty-six years old.

***

BJ and I spent the next day in the city, shopping until we were tired.

"Oh, damn!" I saw the traffic jam too late, as BJ and I had already driven onto the Don Valley Parkway.

"It's too late. We're on it now."

"Pain that it catches us without warning."

"It's only on this side. The other lanes are empty."

"A bad accident?"

"It must be." She paused. "Oh, I see. Look over there."

A police officer had parked his car across an entrance to the southbound lanes and a helicopter flew overhead.

When traffic was flowing well, the DVP was a joy to drive, with its curves and bends and three good lanes in each direction giving it a rhythm. The swaths of daffodils and bluebells had finished blooming for the year, but the trees were bright with the greenery of early summer. In October, the whole valley would be glorious in the reds and golds and rusts of the maple trees.

That day, the traffic was jammed, but only in the northbound lanes. The police officer stood beside his parked cruiser at the base of a ramp on the opposite side, preventing cars from entering the southbound lanes. At the next southbound ramp, there was another officer doing the same thing.

"Yes, of course," BJ and I said it, almost in unison. "How could we forget?"

The northbound lanes travelled slowly, but there was no honking of horns and no changing of lanes. The three southbound lanes were empty. A major highway had fallen silent.

Four police motorcycles approached from the north, then two more, and then motorcycles flanking a police car. All had their lights flashing. Then there were black limousines, then the hearse, followed by more police cruisers and motorcycles. I lost track of the number of vehicles.

When they passed, the northbound traffic started to move again and the southbound lanes filled with their usual traffic. The people on the overpasses took down their flags and began to disburse. Life must always return to normal.

***

Other volcanoes started to rumble. The CBC reported ash from volcanoes in Ecuador and Guatemala. The city of Guayaquil was under an ash cloud. Air space in places other than Europe was closed, disturbing the lives of people in those areas. In Guatemala, two people died because of ash.

The next day, the clouds were soft and the breeze was gentle. Tony left Amber with me, and she annoyed poor Angel. I decided to let both dogs out so that Amber could run and Angel could bask in the sun or walk beside me, as she wished.

While Amber was exploring, Angel and I walked through the garden slowly, watching birds land on and take off from blossoms. There was the tap-tapping sound of woodpeckers and the scent of the last few sprigs of lily of the valley. The scent of lilacs was almost gone, and the fragrance of violets a mere memory, but the sweet smells of honeysuckle and dame's rocket were in their glory.

While Amber chased the shadows of birds flying over us, Angel and I discovered a peony almost smothered by weeds. The blossoms were pale pink, almost white, with a fragrance I had forgotten. What a perfect blossom. Actually, two perfect blossoms. Among all the weeds, I found not just one, but two incredibly perfect peony blossoms. Yes, one to grace my bedside table and the other? Should it be on the dresser? On the bathroom counter? In the kitchen? No. The piano.

I wondered who would pick peony blossoms the following year. In my decluttering to prepare the house for sale, I occasionally wondered who would buy it. Would some other woman find joy in this peony bush or plough it under?

The air was cool. When I put the big tablecloth outside to dry, my skin felt chilled. The leaves of the old catalpa trees moved back and forth, sometimes slowly, sometimes rapidly, depending on the whims of the wind. The birch tree Dan and I planted a few years earlier had already bent, pushed to one side by the prevailing wind, and the main leader of the older birch he planted long before had been snapped by a storm. Our birch tree remained but had been mutilated. The remnants of the mutilated tree stood straight. In some ways, it was more attractive.

The peonies, so magnificent for BJ's party, continued to perfume each room, even though petals fell, littering tables and countertops. While hanging the tablecloth, I looked at the garden. The peony bushes were in full bloom—some of the blossoms held high, and others falling to the ground, felled by wind and rain. Most of the irises had finished their bloom, although there were a few late ones not quite ready to give up their glory. They were surrounded by early daisies, which always reminded me of Roger.

Daisies were the flower loved by my generation, during the time Roger and I marched and went flying. We wore daisies in our hair and at our necks. There were news photos of young American women wearing the same styles I wore and putting daisies into the barrels of guns held by American men, just as young, sent by the authorities to control the people carrying daisies.

I smoothed the tablecloth, trying to ensure that wrinkles would be minor, while looking out at the garden. In the flowerbed just beyond the firepit, the poppies were in bloom. These poppies were in soft colours—pale peach or pink, almost white—and the petals were fluffy.

The paper poppies we wear in November were created to remember another kind of poppy—one with smaller, darker blooms that grows wild on the beaches of Northern France. When Dan and I visited those beaches, I picked wild poppies and pressed them in a book. The beaches were gentle then, and the sounds were of the sea, the cries of gulls, and the voices of children running into the surf; the sea smells were there, on breezes.

***

On the south side of Toronto Island, pointing toward the USA, there is a long boardwalk pier. Couples often buy ice cream cones or hot dogs and then stroll out to the end, where the view to the south is of the lake, with waves in whatever their mood might be and sailboats moving in accordance with the mood of the wind. Sometimes, the wind can be hard, putting anyone at the end of the pier at risk of being blown into the lake. Lovers would hold each other tightly in such a wind.

Roger and I used to walk along the pier, right to the very end, and look out at the lake in its vastness. From the air, the lake had seemed tame and gentle, with sunlight making the waves glitter. At the end of the pier, with the waves surrounding you, the perspective felt different.

The piers at English seaside towns, like Brighton and Eastbourne, were originally built as ferry terminals, as well as for the pleasure of taking the sea air. When they were built taking a ferry to France was a pleasure in itself. Tourists from the continent were welcome, and English ladies went to Paris to see the fashions.

The British government closed the piers at during World War Two, concerned that they might be used by the enemy in some way. They became off limits to strolling couples, but those couples could still enjoy cockles and winkles in paper cones and fish and chips wrapped in yesterday's headlines. Rolls of barbed wired were set out on the beach, in fear of an invasion that never came. When the air raids were over, the people there lost homes and lives.

When Dan and I visited Normandy, we went as tourists. We visited the museum, with its flags waving in a breeze, and we walked along the beach, the skin of our bare feet stepping on places soldiers had fallen. We visited Caen and, being Canadian, asked directions to the military cemetery at Courseulles.

"I wish we had more time," Dan had said. "We should be looking at the American and British graves, too."

"Yes," I answered, thinking of Mum's friend Bruni and wondering whether someone she had loved was buried in the German cemetery.

The forces fighting Germany were British, American, Canadian, Free French, Polish, Australian, and Norwegian. The cemetery at Courseulles felt serene, with closely mown grass and a tidy fence. The graves, marked by the maple leaf, told us of names and ranks and ages of those who are buried there. When Dan and I wandered along the rows, I looked at the ages more than anything else. Most of them were younger than Tony. Many were teenagers, little older than the boys who delivered the telegrams to people waiting for news of individual soldiers. Most were younger than Roger and I were in the days when we flew over Toronto Island.

***

I sorted through papers, agonizing over which to throw away, which to keep, which to give to someone who might find them of interest. Most were thrown away. In the mess of old papers, there were other things. Photographs. An old camera. The instruction manual for another camera.

The camera was an "instamatic," and I remember using it. It was so easy, just point and click and then wind the film forward. We used film in those days. It was always exciting to take a roll of film into the local drug store to have it developed, and then wait the few days it would take to get the photos back. They came with a set of negatives, which was the film itself, after processing.

The instruction manual was for a slightly more sophisticated camera. It must have been the one Roger gave me for Christmas after our first summer of flying.

Old photographs: one of Roger, with unremembered friends, all in matching long hair; and the other of me wearing a long floral skirt and a loose white peasant top, with a crocheted shawl around my shoulders. It must have been a cool day, with just enough wind to blow my hair back from my face.

Here we were, on a weekend in Kingston, he in his usual jeans and jean jacket, me in the same long floral skirt and white peasant blouse. We must have asked someone to click these photos of the two of us, in front of the river, in front of the Martello tower.

The phone interrupted my memories. It was Pat.

"When are you coming over? Do you have your dates yet?"

"Oh, I'm sorry! I really have to get going on that. . . . July looks good for you?"

"Yes, July's fine . . . but, when in July?"

"Your cruise leaves on the twenty-sixth. . . . How much free time do you need beforehand?"

"Well, really . . . I suppose we'd need the twenty-fifth free . . . whatever. So, when are you coming?"

"Right. I have to set dates."

"Yes. You do." She was emphatic.

"Ok."

"When are you going to actually book a flight?" She persisted.

"It might not be a flight."

"What?"

"Surface looks better with that volcano still there."

"Cruises are nice." She became enthusiastic. "David and I have been having a wonderful time on ours. There's so much to do!"

"No. Freighter."

"Oh, nooo! Not that nonsense! Just book the flight!"

**

At the travel agency, I asked the agent about cancellation insurance in case of illness and whether I could cancel for any other reason.

The morning news reported that yet another Canadian soldier had been killed in Afghanistan. He was looking for a cache of weapons when the device exploded. Again, the news told us nothing about other people, military or civilians, who were injured. Was this man looking through a weapons stockpile all by himself? The news told very little about his personal life, though his family may have wanted to maintain privacy. It did tell us his age. He was thirty-five years old.

There were more deaths in Afghanistan after the thirty-five-year-old Canadian. Ten NATO soldiers were killed in one day. Seven were Americans, but the news didn't tell us the details or the nationalities of the others.

There were other things, too: a police training centre in Kandahar was attacked by suicide bombers, there were questions about bribery, and three ISAF members were killed. War goes on.

"So, is it settled?" David asked when I called to verify which dates were convenient for him and Pat.

"Not completely. I still can't find a freighter going at the right time and in the right direction."

"Hah!" He laughed. "You wouldn't really travel by freighter? Would you?"

"Well, what if I'm over there and that ash cloud comes over again?"

"Well, I suppose you'd just stay with us for another day or two. . . . We could even do some extra thing . . . no problem."

I couldn't explain what it was about the ash cloud or the threats from a volcano in Iceland. Perhaps it wasn't the ash cloud at all. Perhaps I just wanted to do something different and have an adventure. No one I know had ever travelled by freighter. To go off on something unusual could be my way of flying, but that would sound silly to David.

"Are you all right?" He sounded concerned by my pause.

"Sure."

"You don't sound it. What's going on?"

"Oh, just getting rid of things. It's a mess, but I'm doing it."

"Well, you can relax with us in July, then."

"Right."

***

I kept burning things. Dan's executor went through the mess with me. The main lesson we learned was to avoid living with a packrat, but if you had to live with one, be the first to die. The books and records and letters went back decades. They had no value, sentimental or otherwise.

"Garbage," he said while pushing off layers of grime and looking at the dates on papers in moldy boxes in the basement.

"True," I agreed. "But confidential garbage."

"Right. If I rent a van, I could cart all this to my office and go through it bit by bit, but I don't really like the idea of having piles of moldy boxes there."

"No. The smell might make your clients wonder about you."

Our solution was to have a strong young man carry the boxes up to the back porch where we could do our lungs a favour by sorting through the boxes in open air. From there, it was a simple matter of pitching most things into a rubbish bin and burning the confidential papers. Easy?

It was not quite as easy as we had thought. Rick, the nice young man who carried the boxes up to the porch, also set a lot of them in a big pile near the firepit, close enough that I could move them, one by one, into the fire, making it more convenient. I got the fire going nicely, just at a slow effective burn. The weather was perfect, with no rain, a slight breeze, but not a strong wind.

When the fire was doing well, I took a break for lunch, sitting by the window while eating my sandwich, happily watching the fire and seeing that all was well. The phone, which was not beside the window, rang.

"Hello."

"Oh, hi."

"It's Grace."

Grace was my real estate agent.

"This is great. I was just getting ready to leave a message. We hardly ever get each other directly. I was just about to ask your answering machine to call my answering machine."

We laughed a bit, as she was right about our usual experience with the telephone.

"You were asking about other things to do before listing. I think it's best to just get it on the market soon . . . as long as the junk is gone and the place is looking good . . ." She explained the realities of changing markets. Economic troubles in Europe could affect the marketability of a house near Toronto. We chatted about various things until the doorbell rang. It was Rick.

"Ummm . . . is it supposed to be like that?" he pointed toward the fire.

"OH, NO!"

The breeze had become more than a breeze, and an ember from the formerly calm fire must have landed on the huge pile of files. Instead of a small gentle fire, we had a small furious fire and a large, threatening fire. I turned on the garden faucet and ran toward the other end of the hose, which was already in the right place.

"Well, you wanted to burn them," he said. "Why not just let it burn?"

"It isn't that simple . . . look!" I pointed toward the papers, all confidential, blowing away from the fire and across the lawn. "Here, keep hosing it down." I handed him the hose and ran to grab wood, stones, garden ornaments, anything to weight down the papers.

Finally, the fire was under control.

By the time the fire was out and papers secured, Rick and I were covered in soot. We washed our hands and faces and drank lots of ice water. Then we laughed about it.

There was a breeze, so I dared not leave the fire and risk watching confidential papers blowing across the lawn, but I let my attention move away from the fire to the beauty around me. Wild canaries flew from branch to branch, in the trees where I had hung feeders filled with niger seed. Niger seed and thistles were their favourites. The thistles, though deemed weeds, attracted beauty in the form of bright little yellow birds. The canaries danced on the branches and in the air, performing acrobatics while flying.

There were clouds, but they were pure white, painted and sculpted against a sky the colour of . . . of what? I can't think of any gemstone worthy of comparison to that sky. There were pleasure planes in the air, dipping their wings, and I thought of Roger.

***

Ah, a lovely email. I was invited to the centennial celebration for the ferry PS *Trillium*. The steam-powered paddle wheeler would leave the ferry terminal at ten thirty in the morning on June 18. The invitation included magic words, inviting me to bypass the ticket booths and go to the prepaid line, using the spell "*Trillium*, City Celebration." It sounded like going to the Land of Oz; on second thought, perhaps it was more like coming back from Oz, by clicking the heels and saying the magic words: "There's no place like home." There would be an unveiling of a plaque and a harbour tour. It was essential to take my camera.

Thoughts of harbour tours, like thoughts of pleasure planes, brought thoughts of Roger again. He was a flyer, and planes always fascinated him far more than boats or any other form of surface travel, but we both loved the harbour.

Did we cross the harbour on the *Trillium*? I couldn't remember. Crossing Toronto Harbour by ferry was both routine and extraordinary. Routine because it was the only way to get to the Island. Extraordinary because it was always so different from being on the mainland. Though short, the crossing seemed long and leisurely.

I had never timed it, but some people say it takes ten minutes; others say fifteen. Perhaps they were not timing the same trips. Boats leaving the same terminal for Ward's Island, Centre Island, or Hanlan's Point had three different destinations, so it would seem logical that there might be three different crossing times. Time felt irrelevant while on the ferry. Although ferries leave and, usually, arrive at a specific time, once on one you have no control. The ferry would carry you to its destination and get you there when it would.

The fire continued the following day, as there was so much to be burned. On every day with a light breeze, I felt aware of how quickly it could change. The length of the garden hose was more than adequate to reach the firepit, so I kept it ready, with the faucet fully open, while I continued to add papers and stir the flames.

After two days of rain, the damp paper smoldered. That could be misleading, the dampness making it difficult to set it afire, but not enough to stop a fire from spreading once set. Flames sometimes die down to almost nothing and sometimes flare up. The pattern was arbitrary and unpredictable.

A small plane flew overhead. It was a strange day for a pleasure flight; there were clouds and the sky was a blend of the same shades of grey as the smoke from the smoldering fire. The clouds kept changing their patterns, layers of dark grey over light and light grey over dark, changing shapes as the wind blew them apart and together again while moving them across the sky.

The plane was the usual size of a pleasure craft, but the pilot was not circling or dipping his wings. The route was a straight line, heading toward the city. There was no way of knowing what purpose that pilot might have, but the directness of the route and the speed of the plane made it clear that he must have one.

I decided to leave the fire to return a bottle to Toma, my neighbour. He always took pride in his homemade wine. He passed bottles around the neighbourhood every Christmas. In my decluttering, I came across an empty one, a beautifully shaped bottle to return to him.

"AH! Come in! Come in!" he said when he saw me walking away from his house after leaving the bottle at the door. "Why do you not come in?"

I went in.

"Here, let me get you a glass of wine." He pulled out a chair for me and placed a glass on the table. "I know I should not say this so much, but I think this is the best wine ever made."

Toma made wine again that year, despite Marija's death. The two of them did everything together, making wine, jams, sauerkraut, pickles, all in the style of the "old country." They grew up in the same village and, despite being small children at the time, never forgot the Nazi occupation.

Occupation forced their families to use every scrap of food, preserving as much as possible, in containers small enough to be easily portable, in case they were forced to move quickly, and easily tradable for whatever else they might need. In Canada, they continued the pattern, but the wine, jams, sauerkraut, and pickles were now made for the pleasure they gave to Toma and Marija and the friends and neighbours who benefitted from their generosity.

"You're right." I sipped the wine. "You can taste the fruit. It's delicious."

"Ya, I think so. . . . This wine is not so strong as the last. . . . This is much better."

It tasted strong to me, but the alcohol went down easily. The clear red wine might be better described as purple.

"Did you use different grapes this year?" I sniffed the perfume.

"AH! Good nose! Your nose has a memory! Yes, Marija thought we should try this. I didn't know what to do. I want to do things just as we always did, but she thought we should try this. She was right. . . . She was always right."

During other visits, he took me on tours of his house, showing beautiful pictures of Marija when she was young and showing the various things that captured her interest. She was beautiful and warm and well educated. His sadness remained evident, but his house was immaculate, and he went on to make the best batch of wine ever.

"But what about you?" he asked.

"Oh, I'm ok."

"Will you stay my neighbour?"

"I don't think so. I need to move on."

"You need to rest."

"Oh, I'm going to; I'm going to England soon. It's to scatter my mum's ashes."

"GOOD! Was that her wish?"

"She didn't say, but I know she'd like it. I have to find the best way to honour her."

"Ah, yes, I did the same with Marija. It's the way it has to be, back to the old country."

"The only problem is that volcano in Iceland."

"Ahh! I know! My plane was in Vienna and I had to wait there. I missed my next flight and it was terrible. Ok in the end, though. I got to our village, and everything was fine."

"Lucky."

"So, when do you fly out?"

"I might not fly."

He stared at me for a moment, obviously waiting for an explanation.
"I'm thinking of surface travel."
"GOOD! A cruise would be a good holiday for you! Much better!"
"Maybe not a cruise."
"How can you go by surface without being on a boat?"
"It's the kind of boat—it would be fun to go by freighter."
He gulped back the rest of his wine.

***

Pat emailed, suggesting a few ideas for my visit. She had arranged a family gathering "for what is left of the family," as she put it. We were also invited to my cousin Kate's house. Kate bought it a few years ago, partly because it is a pleasant house in a nice neighbourhood, and partly because it was the family home. The upstairs bathroom was where Pat used to watch Mum do her makeup.

Pat also asked whether I had ideas about things I'd like to do in London. Yes, of course. I had never been to the Cabinet War Rooms, even though they are so close to the standard "must see" things, like Trafalgar Square and Westminster Abbey. Nor had I visited the museum at Wellington Barracks. They might be worth an afternoon.

I suggested to Pat that she and David and I might also go "total tourist" and spend a day riding a double-decker bus. There was some controversy a few years earlier about a decision to replace the red double-deckers with "bendy" buses. Whether the heads that prevailed were saner or simply more romantic, double-decker buses remained part of London.

On days when we could not fly but wanted to sit together and feel that we were travelling, Roger and I would ride the Queen Street car. The streetcars, along Queen and College, and up Parliament and Spadina, were the old-fashioned ones, travelling on rails and connected by tall poles to the electric lines above. The distinctive clicking sound of their wheels and the dinging of their bells were part of life in our city. When there were noises from City Hall that they should be eliminated and replaced with modern buses, the outcry was similar to the London reaction to the elimination of double-deckers. They were the way Roger and I would explore Toronto from the ground, just as Edith and Harald travelled through London on the upper decks of red buses.

There were more boxes on the porch to sort through. The fires were burning again, and my lungs hurt. It was ridiculous to expose myself to the smoke and soot, but some things had to be burned. Sometimes, it seemed easier to just pitch everything into the rubbish bin, but that would be a mistake.

There were boxes of old books. My first thought was to simply throw them into the bin. The musty smell was overwhelming, and I didn't want them in the house. Despite the odour and the bugs crawling over them, I couldn't resist opening those boxes to see what I was tossing.

Ah, yes, a box of books from my first year of university. An introduction to English poetry, my personal collection of favourite poems, a reading list chosen by a professor who felt that no one could be well read without becoming familiar with everything on the list, the third edition of *The Concise Cambridge History of English Literature*. I wonder how many editions have been published since?

There were other things in the musty box. Old notebooks? No, not just notebooks, but diaries. They were the records of my life in the 1960s and 70s. The smell seemed less intense, and the bugs less disturbing. The box became welcome to return to my house.

There were lines about Roger and the Island airport and his plane. I had forgotten that it had a name, and he never referred to it as "it." The plane was Akasha, a Sanskrit name meaning "open air" or "space". The musty diary described going up into the open air with Roger, with Akasha carrying us into a place of freedom and space.

***

What a lovely day! *Trillium* celebrated her one-hundredth birthday with dignitaries, the mayor, a cabinet minister, media people, historians, and . . . well, the guest list wasn't quite clear, but it was an honour to be on it.

The official time for first boarding was ten thirty, so I rushed to be at the ferry docks by nine. It was a bit silly, but it gave time to go around the area, clicking a few photos. Too many of them included the G-20 barricades.

Our lovely city was chosen to host the 2010 G-20 meetings. The security perimeter took over much of the most beautiful parts of Toronto. Waste disposal containers near the harbour were replaced by plastic bags taped to lamp standards, and the nicest hotels were surrounded by barricades. The barricades were concrete at the base, topped by a mesh made of strands far too thick to be described as "wire." Police officers stood at the openings of the barricades, although there was nothing indicating that I was not allowed to simply walk past the police officers.

All of that disappeared once aboard *Trillium*. The old paddle ship took us back to another era, another century, when men tipped their hats and ladies bowed their heads. A full century has gone by, but *Trillium* steamed on.

While looking at displays showing timelines and old photos, I realized that Roger and I never crossed the harbour on *Trillium*; during that time period she was out of service, left to sink and rot, abandoned in a lagoon and almost forgotten. Dan and I never boarded *Trillium* either, which seemed strange, as he was so fond of boats and boating. *Trillium*, after one hundred years, was still being discovered.

One of the special guests was an elderly man in a suit. When I offered to get a drink for him, he declined but struck up a conversation.

"People don't know enough about the harbour," he told me. "That airport over there . . . lots of history."

"Oh, yes, you mean Little Norway."

"Yes, the Norwegians were there. . . . There were aerodromes all across Canada during that war."

"Really?"

"Yes, all across . . . all the Allies came here to train the pilots. We had Aussies and Kiwis and Free French and Norwegians and everybody else."

"Are the aerodromes still there?"

"Oh, some are, some aren't. People like to forget the bad things." He paused before going on. "Thousands of them died in training."

I chose to avoid asking for details about that part. His facial expression suggested personal memories. Changing the topic seemed safer.

"Isn't it lovely to see this boat restored?"

"It is," he agreed. "Always nice to see the old things come back in good ways. I know the lakes. Before I joined the navy, I was on a freighter for two years."

"A freighter? On the lakes?"

"Yes, right from Lake Superior to Toronto."

Now, that was an interesting chat. Here was a man who had actually been on a freighter. I was slightly envious but didn't say so. The whole day reminded me how much I enjoy boat rides.

***

Rick, the nice young man with muscles, finished pulling the basement debris up from below and decided to set the surface of my life into some semblance of order. He did well. Doors were painted or replaced, weeds attacked, stair railings installed, the garage emptied, and everything cleaned. Rick had an eye for these things. He laughed when I asked when he and his wife would be free to join me for dinner, but I was serious. I hoped they both liked pizza, heated up from store-bought frozen. If I added a salad and a bottle of wine, it could be a meal, and I wanted to invite them.

After he left, I went out to the garden. There had to be someone out there, some couple who could love the house as it deserved to be loved. He would enjoy a garden, she would raise horses, and they would both want to entertain. She would cook, he would play billiards, and they would keep a full bar. Those were my hopes and dreams for the house.

Hopes and dreams are part of the future, and we do not know the future. We know only the past, its happy times as well as sad, and the present with all its complexity.

I poured a glass of wine and wandered out to examine the late peonies and early roses. Yes, clip a rose for my bathroom bud vase, light pink and very fragrant, a rose of great charm. Yes, a peony blossom, perfect for my mother's bud vase, which would look nice on the kitchen counter, where I would see it more frequently.

The greenhouse was my playhouse in an earlier time. I planted and potted there and dreamed of new growth. None of those dreams ever quite came true, but they were worth dreaming. After Rick carted away the debris of my dreams, I returned to the greenhouse to see what was left.

There was still beauty. Yes, the structure was still solid and the windows needed nothing more than a spray of water to let the light in again.

Something in a corner caught my eye. A piece of rope? A coil of wire? It moved, then disappeared into the stones. Even then, in that beautiful place cleansed of debris, there were snakes.

***

"What's going on?"

It was Pat.

"Hi. Where are you? I thought you were on a cruise?"

"We are. The boat stopped in Oslo for a day, so I thought I'd call.... We've seen some horrible pictures on the news."

"The G-20? Yep. It's been pretty bad. Windows smashed, lots of arrests, a police car burning at King and Bay, and they even had to close the Eaton Centre."

"NO! That closes off the shopping!"

"At least it's over."

"Oh, I know what it's like; we had it in London, too."

"The CBC played a farewell song today, Ray Charles singing 'Hit the Road, Jack, and don't you come back no more, no more.' I loved it!"

"Yes. So, when are you hitting the road?"

"Hmm?"

"The air, rather . . . when are you coming over?"

"Oh. Right. I have to get going on that. I still haven't found a freighter."

"Nooo! No more of that nonsense." She sounded determined. "I'm booking a flight for you."

"But I'm not sure about—"

"I'm booking it. Now . . . I must dash. We're on a tour, and both David and the guide are glaring at me. Bye."

She was gone. Just like that, without even waiting for my reply.

I had an email later: *"Flight booked. David will meet you at Gatwick. You arrive on the 7th. Love, Pat."*

She didn't even consider the dangers of the Icelandic volcano. She can be a lot like Mum sometimes.

I wondered how they enjoyed Oslo. It's a small city, but it looks beautiful. Maybe the smallness is part of the charm.

Norway is part of the NATO team in Afghanistan, too. Four Norwegian soldiers were killed that weekend. Part of my mind thought, *Four of theirs*, but another part thought, *Four of ours*.

***

Peonies faded, and roses bloomed. The flight Pat booked was just two days away, making me unsure whether to be happy about already having my passport. Forgetting to get one would have meant I couldn't go. There was still so much to do: the lawn mower broke down, the grass was long, there was more to declutter, and the house was a mess.

Mum's portrait and the urn of her ashes were on a bookshelf in the den. Dried flowers from her memorial service were on both the urn and the portrait. They dried nicely, and the colours remained clear—soft mauve and pink roses—with baby's breath and ferns and some pink things that still looked very pretty.

The portrait overlooked the jeans I had left on the back of a chair, the aging magazines on the coffee table, and the underwear and pantyhose on the floor, but the eyes were not looking at those; they were looking somewhere else, as though other things might be more important.

She must have been about twenty-five when that picture was taken. She had photos taken in a few poses, all to be used as postcards to send to men of various nationalities—Belgian, Dutch, Norwegian. There may even have been an Englishman or two.

She was the classic beauty queen of that era, with dainty features, cupid's bow lips, groomed eyebrows, all in the look of a china doll. The portrait was to the right of the urn, containing her ashes. On the left there was another china doll. The doll's face looked a lot like my mother. There is delicacy and perhaps a bit of sadness. The hair, eyebrows, and cheeks and nose, lips, and chin were flawless, like Mum's.

The doll's eyes were looking to the side, like my mother's, but there was a difference. The doll's eyes looked to the side and down; my mother's eyes looked up. My mother was strikingly beautiful, but the delicate look of her facial features was misleading. She was strong.

***

Two days passed too quickly. I had to be at the airport that afternoon. I still had to do laundry. The things I wanted to take were a bit rumpled, and some needed to be washed. There was no laundry soap; I had to dash off to the store to get some.

Laundry soap. Fabric softener. Bleach. The soap goes into the washer, not the dryer. The bleach goes into the little thing on the side, not just over the clothes sitting in the machine. The fabric softener goes in at the end. Yes, I could have it all done and all packed in time.

Did I have everything? Black trousers. White trousers. Three tops. Two sweaters. Simple black dress. Black shoes. Tennis shoes. Sandals. Bathing suit. Lots of underwear. Nightgown. Dressing gown. I was forgetting something, but what?

Oh, yes, the ashes! I couldn't forget that little container!

Something else? Ah, Mum's favourite ring. The band was yellow gold, and it had emeralds and diamonds. It could be resized for Pat.

Yes, I could have everything packed and ready when the limo arrived.

The limo was early. My bags were packed and near the door, but I forgot to look for shoes for the trip. The driver was patient while I ran from room to room to find them. By that time, he had loaded my bags. I locked the door and was ready to get into the limo, but he held up a hand to stop me.

"My name is Anton, and I am your driver."

"Yes?"

"Do you have your tickets?"

"Yes."

"Passport?"

"Yes."

"Medication, if needed?"

"None needed."

"Good." He paused. "List of addresses for people who should be sent postcards?"

"No postcards needed."

"Fine. We are not finished yet." He held his hand up again, in a stop signal. "Gifts for people you will visit?"

"Yes."

"*All* the gifts? For *all* the people you will visit?"

"You have done this before, haven't you?"

"Oh, yes. I have. Many times. So, what is the answer?"

"To what?"

"To my question. *All* the gifts? For *all* the people you will visit?"

"Yes to both questions."

"Have you turned off the lights you should turn off?'

"Yes."

"Turned on the lights you should turn on?"

"Yes."

"Turned off the stove?"

"Yes."

"The coffee maker?"

"Yes."

He paused. He examined me, the house, and then his feet before he gave his verdict.

"We are ready to go."

It dawned on me that he forgot to ask whether I had remembered to bring cremated human remains.

***

Flights were scheduled in military time, and I miscalculated by an hour, arriving at the gate just as they were boarding. At least, I got my window seat.

The man beside me kept moving his arm over my armrest and changing the channel on the sound system. The meal had something to do with chicken. Other than that, it wasn't definable. Paying for a neck rest was a complete waste of money, as sleep was impossible while the man who changed audio channels also fidgeted even when the movie wasn't playing. There was also a child behind me who was so excited by flying that he kept kicking his little feet right against the back of my seat. Moving forward didn't help, as the woman ahead of me had her chair reclined as far back as it could go.

At least the plane was in the air, and there had been no reports of Icelandic ash for some time. I was on the way to London and had lost all hope of having a ride on a freighter.

When I decided to stop my futile attempts at sleep, I lifted the window blind to enjoy the view. The view, after all, was the reason I paid the few extra dollars for the window seat.

There was no view. I saw nothing but clouds. I had hoped to see coastline and imagine what might be beneath us. There must always be coast or land or sea beneath us, but whatever it was couldn't be revealed while clouds were obscuring everything.

There was light above the clouds The thickness of the clouds showed how dark it must have been below, but there was always sunlight on the upper level. The clouds looked light and fluffy and so benign, even though they were creating darkness below.

Weather over the English Channel changes quickly. A morning of mist or rain could turn sunny before noon, and the sunny noon might be followed by afternoon cloud. The weather is shared by people on both sides of the Channel, so a pilot flying over the cliffs on the South Coast of England knows what to expect in Northern France or the Low Countries. Pilots on missions to take photographs had mixed feelings about clouds. The breaks in clouds revealed the things to be photographed, but they also revealed the location of the pilot's plane.

Sometimes, soaring upward in Akasha, Roger and I would sing. Akasha made her own music, with the whir of the engines and the whooshing of air over the wings. Her music inspired us. I remember Roger singing "Both Sides Now" while flying. It was Joni Mitchell's big hit that year.

I sang with him, and we felt that we had "looked at clouds from both sides now." We hadn't, really. Even though we knew Ken and other Americans, and were aware of My Lai and Kent State, and the power of the Ku Klux Klan, those problems were not ours. We cared enough to carry signs and organize rallies, but our suffering was from a distance, and by our choice. We had seen more of "bows and flows of angel hair, and ice cream castles in the air" than of the darkness below. We had seen only the illusions of clouds, as Joni Mitchell described in the song..

After all my concern about ash clouds and the discomfort caused by a man who kept changing audio channels and a child who kept kicking the back of my seat, the plane landed smoothly. At first, all the bags coming down the conveyor belt looked the same, except for one in hot pink and another in yellow with purple flowers, so finding my dark grey one could have been be a challenge, but there it was, easily retrievable.

When I clicked my carryon bag to the suitcase, I was delighted to see that I was one of very few travellers who had matching pieces, colour coordinated to their clothing, looking rather chic. A quick trip to the ladies'—to splash my face, brush my hair, and renew lipstick—made me feel ready for anything.

"Is this the right line?" a woman asked me, obviously recognizing a knowledgeable traveller.

"I certainly hope so, as I am joining it," I answered with a smile.

We chatted about London while in the customs and immigration queue. A woman at the front directed people to "number four" or "number two," keeping everyone moving. We reached her after about half an hour of pleasant chat, with me giving my new companion tips about what to see in London. The woman directing people to officials under numbers glanced at our passports and noticed the blue colour.

"Canadians over there," she said. "You're in the wrong queue."

The woman I had been chatting with looked at me in a way that made me feel she would not bother to make notes about my tips on what to do in London. We joined the other queue, which held us in place for another half hour. After that, it was easy.

"What is the purpose of your trip?" The Customs officer was businesslike but pleasant.

"A family visit."

"How long will you be here?"

"A little over two weeks."

"Welcome to the UK. Enjoy your visit." The customs officer gave a warm smile.

There they were, my aunt and uncle, smiling and waving as soon as I had gone through the big door. Pat had let her hair go grey and it was like my mother's—fine, silky silver, setting off the blueness of her eyes. David was as tall as ever; his hair was grey, too, but there was less of it.

"HELLO!" They continued to wave and smile, and I couldn't resist running toward them. We embraced over the barrier rope and then moved along, parallel to it. Our hugs were interrupted only by the hugs exchanged by other people.

"We saw when you landed," Pat said. "You got through quickly."

"No one asked me about liquids, gels, or human remains."

"What?"

"Nothing. I thought I might have to explain Mum's ashes."

"You don't have them floating around in your handbag, do you?"

"No. I just wondered whether I had to declare human ashes."

"Oh, don't be silly. If they don't ask, don't tell, and that isn't a standard question." Pat then began to chatter about plans and continued the chatter until we reached the car, when David took control. He heaved my bags into the boot of his car.

"Heavy!" he commented, and I simply nodded.

While we were getting out of the airport parking lot and onto the roads, Pat resumed her chatter about plans. "Darling, I think we should take Sarah to that lovely tandoori place."

"Will we have time with everything else you've planned?"

"Do you like Indian food?" she asked.

"Yes, and the spicier the better."

"It isn't all that spicy. It's just delicious." She paused briefly. "Oh, Sissinghurst will be lovely at this time of year, and we think you would like Hever Castle. It's where Henry the Eighth courted Anne

Boleyn. . . ." She left no space for anyone else to comment. ". . . and the family will be over. . . . David, that reminds me . . . I think we're all right for brandy, but we might need more gin."

"Is Margaret coming?"

"Yes."

"Oh, well then, I'll certainly pop out for more gin."

It seemed strange to be a passenger on the left side of the car. As David drove and Pat talked, I thought about the newness of old things, stone walls and hedges of hydrangeas and lavender, along with the happy familiarity of people I so rarely see. Arrival at the house came almost as a surprise.

"Oh, look! We're here already!" I was amazed at how quickly we arrived.

"It isn't a long drive, and she keeps it busy with chattering." David glanced over with a gentle look.

"Oh, nonsense! I don't chatter!"

David and I smiled at each other while he took my suitcase out of the boot and carried it into the house.

"I'll take this up to your room while the two of you decide what to do next. That won't be hard for you, Sarah, as she has so many things planned." He winked.

"Oh, don't be daft! It's all up to Sarah. Come and have a look at the garden; it's lovely right now." She took my arm and led me through the kitchen and into the back garden.

Blue hydrangeas were in their glory against the grey stone wall at the back. Birds flew from the feeder, startled when we walked onto the lawn.

"David does all this himself. Isn't it marvellous?"

"Yes, it is rather." David joined us, with a tray of tea. "I enjoy doing it."

"What is this?" I noticed small pink flowers above low foliage.

"Oh, that's London Pride," Pat answered. "It's a weed, really."

"Oh, I wouldn't call it a weed, but it is very easy to grow," David added. "Noel Coward wrote a song about it during the war. It's tough and survives all sorts of things. Resilient and all that."

"After our tea, we must go over your plans," Pat insisted.

"Haven't you already done that? When we were in the car?" David asked.

"Yes, but Sarah needs to jot things down. The time will go quickly, and she won't want to miss out on anything."

"I'm really here about Mum's ashes."

"Yes. Yes, of course. There has to be more than that, though. Relax today so you'll be rested up."

***

After dinner we sat at the kitchen table, sipping coffee, with the newspaper open to crossword puzzles. Before we started a crossword, David left the room and returned with a tray with three snifters of brandy.

"The real thing. It's cognac. We pick it up whenever we go over the Channel."

"Oh, yes, we do enjoy going over. Would you like to pop over to France while you're here? The Chunnel makes it ever so easy."

"Yes, that sounds like fun."

"Well, here's to fun in France!" Pat raised her snifter in a toast. "Now, what's the word we need?"

"A five-letter word for liquid or gas." David was in charge of calling out the questions.

"Oh, that's too easy!" Pat laughed. "It's 'fluid.'"

"Right. Now then, five letters, beginning with U, meaning below."

"That's too obvious! It's 'under.'"

"Is this how the Brits sell more newspapers?" I asked.

"It is for this house." David gave me his gentle smile.

We finished the crossword puzzle and went on to other puzzles, progressively more challenging. Pat ended the games by announcing that we had to make plans for Saturday.

"The family will be over in the afternoon. You go up to London on Friday while we do a bit of shopping. Salads, I think, with lots of cold things. If the weather is nice, we can set up a buffet in the garden." Pat was always well organized.

"Everything from Waitrose?" David asked.

"I think so. They're good about a loan of glasses, and they do party things well."

"What numbers should I give them?"

"Oh, I don't know. It's just the family." She shrugged, as though it was obvious.

"That could be quite a crowd."

***

The walk to the train station took me past hydrangea hedges and stone walls and along cobbled paths. The station was in a village, now surrounded by housing estates, but retaining its village feel. The restaurants started their preparation early in the day, so the smells of curry and jerk spice mingled with lavender and roses.

The trains looked modern, the old compartments being mere memory, but the commuters were timeless. Some look tired, nodding off to sleep even while going into the city to work. Most read papers, looking at sections on fashion or finance or current affairs.

As we approached Victoria Station, the fumes grew stronger. The mixture of fuel, dirt, and dust with the odours of London reminded me that the train was real; this wasn't a Disney set or an exciting dream.

The commuters dashed off the train and rushed forward in the manner of commuters everywhere. Even those who had been slipping into sleep on the train were soon wide awake, rushing into the city to go about their day.

I stood back, letting the crowd push by me. Then, after the mad rush, I moved forward, deciding not to stop at the coffee stand, and went to the exit gates. David had loaded an Oyster card, the magical card that gives access to all London transit, thereby giving access to all of London. The moment my Oyster card touched the reader, the gates opened and I stepped into London

Even though Victoria station has changed over the generations, it still retains an aura of another time. It serves eighty million people annually, including not only the daily commuters, but travellers from major international airports, tourists, theatre goers, school groups on day trips, people visiting friends and families, and anyone with an interest in seeing London. The station is a fascinating mix of old and new. It's a convenient place to meet a friend for coffee, as it is central and serves so many travel routes. There are cheese and wine shops, clothing stores, book stores, flower and jewellery vendors, Boots pharmacy, and a Marks and Spencer's food shop.

Caution was in order as I left the building, as there were so many buses. Once past the buses, I could walk along Buckingham Palace Road, toward the palace itself, to arrive at the corner across the street from St. James' Park and Wellington Barracks.

My temptations while walking along Buckingham Palace Road were embarrassing, even to myself. Every postcard drew my hand toward it. Some of the patterns of the china cups and saucers would fit the decor of my house, and some would fit Pat and David's. How could I walk past them? The tea towels were pretty, too, and would be nice to have. Would it be better to buy one with a picture of a London bus or a picture of Big Ben? Which is more "London"? Why not both? On the other hand, did I need more tea towels? I bought chocolates instead, wrapped in pretty papers with pictures of the Royals. They were for friends, but perhaps I could have one or two.

There was a huge crowd in front of the palace, watching the changing of the guard. The new guard had arrived, and the old would march back to Wellington Barracks. I decided to follow them, but at a slow stroll, to see the chapel.

The Guards' Chapel had been restored, but not as it was before the bombing. There was a look of tradition about the place, and a look of modernity. Past and future meet at the altar. Some military group left music stands at the front, with sheet music still in place. I saw the memorials to those who were killed, but there was also music.

Reaching for another chocolate, I looked into the bag to find only wrappers. Perhaps my friends would enjoy something else. I had eaten most of the Royal family.

I wandered through the chapel and then across the road to St. James' Park, stopping on the bridge over the pond and watching children running after birds. The lawns were well kempt, despite the many feet that walked over them. The park ends at Horse Guards Road, with

Horse Guards Parade and government offices on the other side. There were signs for various things, but the one that caught my eye was for the Cabinet War Rooms. The War Rooms had been converted to a museum, showing life as it was inside during wartime. In all my years of visiting London, I had never seen that museum.

The Cabinet War Rooms are underground in the City of Westminster, near Number 10 Downing Street. The new entrance is for tourists; the original was unseen by passersby. Descending into the Cabinet War Rooms was easy in some ways but frightening. They were dimly lit and cramped. I noticed some small rooms had army bunks, and even the rooms used by the prime minister and Mrs. Churchill were small and near the galley area, with stacks of pots and pans that must have created noise as well as odours of fish and cabbage.

The map room was as central as the Cabinet Room itself. Pins marked the changing positions of the fronts. Some pins moved forward, toward the enemy, some moved back, in retreat. There were times when there was no movement at all, and other times when the pins were taken out and placed in new positions as rapidly as information could flow.

There was an alcove with several desks. On one desk, there were two sugar cubes, brown with age, and a sign explaining that the officer at that desk forgot to take them when the war ended.

After seeing the Cabinet War Rooms, I went to the British Library, which had an exhibition about maps, and had named it "Power, Propaganda, and Art." Old maps, and new ones, showed the world as the mapmakers, or the people paying the mapmakers, wished it to be. Some old maps showed terra incognita, in acknowledgement of mystery, and lands yet to be explored and, ultimately, conquered by the people paying the mapmaker. The maps showed their patron's home, and by extension the patron, as the centre of the world.

***

While we were drinking our coffee after Saturday breakfast, David opened the paper to the crossword puzzle, as usual.

"Seven letters, beginning with B, meaning an ephemeral globe."

"Too easy. It's 'bubble,' but we don't have time for that this morning." Pat was dismissive of the crossword.

"Why not?"

"You know why not. We have to get ready for later."

"Don't we already have everything?" he asked. "I got the gin."

"We're not set up. You two get things ready in the garden while I sort the food."

David put away the paper, and we cleared the table and washed the dishes. Then David and I went out to the garden.

"She'll want chairs everywhere. I know her! I'll set up the tables; you pull out the chairs. We'll set them all out and then rearrange them the way she directs." He gave a gentle laugh.

"Where should I put them?"

"It doesn't really matter. Just put them wherever. Even if we have things in perfect order, she'll come out and insist on something else. Just watch."

We carried tables and chairs to the corners of the garden, setting some in shade and some in sun, placing the chairs in threes and fives for conversation. There were already three chairs in the gazebo, so we left it as it was. Pat came out just as we had finished.

"David, don't you think it would be nice if we had a little sitting area off to that side?"

David turned to me and whispered, "There. Didn't I tell you?"

David and I followed Pat's hand gestures to rearrange the tables and chairs, following her as though she were conducting an orchestra. By one thirty, everything had been rearranged.

"Yes, that's better. Shall we go back to the crossword?" She was happy with the changes and ready to relax.

"Yes. Come on, Sarah, your aunt is giving us a bit of time off."

***

We had finished three crossword puzzles and were sipping tea when the doorbell rang.

"Someone a bit early?" Pat wondered. "Either that or a stranger. Why don't you get it, Sarah? You'll either meet one of your relatives or be asked to convert to some strange religion."

The door opened before I touched it, and an old man, standing straight despite the need for two canes, pushed in, followed by a woman about my age.

"Uncle Peter! And Jess! You both look well."

"All well for an old man who gets dragged about by a daughter. Now, where's my hug?"

The hugging was enthusiastic and generous.

"Was the flight horrid?" Jess asked.

"Oh, not bad. Just the usual boredom, but it got me here and now I can see you in person."

"It's been far too—" Jess tried to start a conversation.

"Enough of that!" Uncle Peter stopped us. "Let me have a look at you. Ah, yes, you have your mum's face. Not as pretty, mind you, but the same general shape."

"Don't mind Dad," Jess apologized.

"I don't mind at all."

"Your mum had the most perfect face of any woman I have ever seen." He went on, as though neither Jess nor I had said anything. "She knew how to use it, too. She used to drag me off to dances and then toss me away as soon as she set her sights on some young man. She was always dragging me about that way. Humiliating!" He paused and moved toward the kitchen.

David was coming toward us, to greet the first guests.

"How are you, Peter?" He reached out his hand.

"All very well for an old man, but I'd be better with a drink." Peter ignored the hand. "Where is it?"

"Coming right up. What about you, Jess?"

"Perhaps a bit later. I have to keep an eye on Dad."

"Where's that son of mine? Daughter here did the driving. Has he shown up yet?"

"He will, Dad; we're early."

Uncle Peter stood tall, using his canes for support but not bending down. His personality filled the house, leaving Jess smiling, even while she was left behind.

The family arrived in twos and threes and groups of five. Uncle Peter's son, George, arrived with his wife and children. Uncle Jimmy's teenaged grandsons, Terry and Billy, greeted the adults and answered the usual questions about school and sports, chatting just long enough to be polite, and then went to the other room to play table tennis. Aunt May's grandchildren, and other distant cousins who had not seen each other for years, embraced and continued as though they had met for lunch the day before. Some were children of the aunts and uncles of the generation before mine, but they were all one family. In theory, they were there to see me; in reality, I was simply the catalyst, providing a reason for a family reunion.

They chattered and laughed and showed each other pictures of babies and gardens and dogs, moving the chairs into patterns neither David nor Pat had planned. Drinks were spilled and linens stained, but it didn't matter. Jess and George challenged Terry and Billy to lawn bowls, and lost to them.

They hugged each other and chatted while David offered drinks. Teenagers played games while older people sat and chatted. When the sun started to go down, the party broke up and people hugged each other as they left. Uncle Peter and Jess were the last to leave, with Uncle Peter complaining that he wanted to stay longer.

We packed the glasses into boxes and put most of the party things away quickly. Everything was easily done with three people working together. We relaxed with snifters of cognac and the crossword puzzle before going to bed. There were just a few details to finish the next morning, so we spent most of that morning enjoying coffee in the gazebo.

"What are you doing next?" Pat asked.

"I still need to do something with Mum's ashes, and there's something else, too."

"What's that?"

"I've had an email from an old friend. It's vague, but there has been a death in his family."

"Does he need you in some way?"

"I'm not sure. He's in London and wants to meet for coffee."

"Invite him here. We can do better than coffee."

"It's a bit of a problem. He only has two days and has lots of appointments."

***

The walk to the train station had become a routine part of my day, as though I had never left England. Neighbours recognized me and waved to me, not as a stranger but as someone they knew, even though we had never spoken and we didn't know each other's names. Despite the familiarity, it lost none of its charm, and the ride to Victoria Station lost none of its excitement. Placing my Oyster card on the reader and walking through the gate and into London was as thrilling as ever.

I knew exactly where to find Ken, past the shops near the gates, and across from the timetable boards. He was sitting in the predictable chair, at the coffee shop, looking out at the arrival area. He rose and greeted me with a hug.

"It seems so odd to see you here." I couldn't think of anything else to say.

"But we are both here, so why not? I thought it would be nice to see an old friend in a new place."

"The place isn't new to me."

"Maybe not, but it's a new place for us to see each other."

I couldn't resist returning his smile. "You said you were busy, with lots of things to do."

"Yes, but they haven't chained me to a desk. At least, not yet."

"You said you have to go to Germany. What is it about your Oma? Is she sick?"

"Not exactly. Her sister just died, and it's a bad time for her."

"Of course. That's a bad time for anyone."

"There is a bit more to it. It's the anniversary of her older brother's death.'

"Wasn't that a long time ago?"

"Yes, but it's still painful, and she's still bothered. There was some kind of shame about the brother, but I don't know the details." He looked baffled.

"You have me on edge. What was it?"

"No one talked about it, so I'm just guessing. His widow engraved a swastika on the tombstone, so that tells us a lot."

"Ah, the family Nazi," I nodded. "That would be a good reason to be ashamed of him. Was he horrible?"

"Probably. He was a policeman, and policemen all followed the same leader. I don't like to even think about a guy like that, but it was really hard on Oma. She kept quiet about him."

"I can see that it's hard on you, too. He's dead, and all that is in the past. He can't hurt anyone now."

"No, but things were hard on his widow. Oma's side of the family stayed close and helped her out."

Thoughts of Nazis left us feeling gloomy, so we agreed to be tourists. We took the tube to Westminster, crossed the bridge and went for a ride on the London Eye. We laughed at the details below, of people cycling across the bridge, of parents showing their children the statues, of people on the decks of the tour boats on the Thames. We imagined the people on those boats looking out at us on the London Eye just as we were looking back at them.

After dinner that evening David poured brandy and Pat opened the paper to the crossword puzzle. It was a long summer afternoon, extending into the evening, with light surrounding us.

While David carried the brandy snifters and Pat unfolded the paper, she asked the obvious question. "Did you have a nice time with your friend?"

"He was more Dan's friend than mine, although I did know him before I met Dan."

"It must have been nice to get together."

"It was, but it was strange. He learned his family secret."

"Which was?" David asked while offering the brandy.

"His mother's family were from a little village in Bavaria, and his great uncle was a Nazi."

"I should imagine quite a few people were," Pat pointed out. "Did he do horrible things?"

"He was a policeman, so the answer is probably yes. He was probably brutal."

"Bloody Nazis!"

"Have you thought any more about the ashes?" Pat changed the subject.

"Yes, but I still haven't decided. I can't think of anything that seems right."

"Beachy Head." She gave no explanation.

"What?"

"Beachy Head. It's right beside Eastbourne."

"And we're taking you there anyway," David added.

"And it's lovely . . ." she said.

"And the RAF flew over Beachy Head during the War."

"So, if we're taking you there anyway, you might as well bring along the ashes."

***

The road to Eastbourne goes through the Ashdown Forest, less a forest than a magical place of open woodland, meadows, and streams, and known to children as the Hundred Acre Wood, explored by Winnie the Pooh and his friends. At a certain time of year, it transforms into bluebell woods, with soft blue covering the ground. The gorse nearly always shows bright yellow flowers.

Pat explained the saying, "When gorse is out of bloom, kissing is out of season." Kissing is never out of season. As we drove along the road, the trees enclosed the car in some places, giving the impression there were no other cars and the woods were a place of privacy. Soon after, we drove through small towns and smaller villages, all with stone walls and flowers.

The pier at Eastbourne was visible as we approached, jutting out into the sea and pointing toward France, a reminder of the days of pleasure boats travelling between the two countries. I could see the long promenade following the seafront from the pier to the western end of the town, with the English Channel to the south and a long road, the Grand Parade, with carpet beds in full flower, to the north. There were tents and vendors on the promenade, with shoppers going from one to another.

"Oh, look! It's the European market! I had forgotten it would be here. David, we must take Sarah down here as soon as we've settled in."

"Shouldn't we think about Mum's ashes?" I asked.

"Of course, but she wouldn't mind. She'd approve of the shopping!"

We bought Italian scarves, Spanish olives, French lace, and German cheeses before sampling English wine and honey. We stayed at the market until late afternoon, and then realized the time.

"We'll have to get these things packed away," David pointed out. "Best do that before dinner."

In the evening, we strolled along the promenade, which seemed strangely quiet after the market had left. The sounds were of the sea and the wind and the gulls. We walked to the end of the pier and looked west toward Beachy Head.

"So, will that be the place?" Pat asked.

"For what?"

"The ashes."

"Yes, I suppose so, but it seems so final."

"The finality has already happened."

"Right. So, yes, that will be the place."

"Tomorrow?" David wanted a decision.

"Yes."

"You two go up. The hill's a bit steep for me," Pat explained. "You should know a few things, though. It's a suicide magnet, and people keep throwing themselves off the cliff or falling off."

"She's right. We keep hearing statistics."

"You also need to know the winds are strong, and if it blows the wrong way, you could end up with a face full of ash or become one of the statistics." She said it seriously, and David nodded.

"Oh, great. Just my kind of choice," I replied.

"Let's just go up and see which way the wind blows." David offered the best suggestion.

**

The next morning, David and I left Pat at a tea shop near Beachy Head and walked the narrow path to the top. There were more narrow paths, crossing a large open field north of the path. The wind came in gusts, sometimes strong, sometimes weak, and the dominant direction was indefinable. Perhaps it was because it was a strange day, or perhaps it was simply because we were at the top of a cliff overlooking the sea. The grass and small bushes swayed, not in one direction but to every compass point. A man to the north of us ran with his dog, and then stopped to throw a stick for the dog to fetch. The dog chased the stick, ran in a circle, looking for the stick, then found it and ran back to the master. The two played together while we watched.

"Last week a man fell off the cliff while he was looking for his dog." David looked at me with concern.

"Yes, we do have to be careful. Let's go on a bit."

"This wind is bad."

"It seems to come from all directions."

"Unpredictable," he pointed out. "Are you sure about this?"

"Not really, but . . ." I saw a narrow side path from the main path to the cliff. "What about here?"

"You wouldn't want to step out there, would you?" He stepped back, as though imagining the possible effects of stepping forward.

"No, but . . ."

At that moment, the wind stopped. In the stillness, I opened the container and stepped toward the edge of the cliff, throwing the ashes out and up into the air, toward France. A slight breeze picked them up, and they went up and out, over the English Channel, in a soft grey puff, disappearing against the soft grey of the clouds.

**

We had accomplished our mission and I had seen Eastbourne and Beachy Head. The next morning, back at the house, we sat at the kitchen table, drinking coffee, while David fiddled with another crossword puzzle.

"A seven-letter word, beginning with N, meaning significant or uncommon."

"'Nothing'?" I asked. "No, the meaning doesn't work . . ."

"'Noteworthy'?" Pat wondered.

"No, it has to be seven letters. Still, 'noteworthy' would have the right meaning. . . . What about 'notable'?"

"Ahhh!"

We were congratulating ourselves on 'notable' when the phone rang. Pat went to the den and returned almost immediately.

"For you." She smiled in my direction.

"Me? Who on earth could it be?"

"Some man named Ken something."

When I returned to the kitchen, they asked questions with their facial expressions. They said nothing and I said nothing until Pat broke the silence.

"So—why did you do that?"

"Do what?"

"Your whole body stopped moving. . . . Why?"

"Oh, nothing."

"Something, I think. What was it?"

"Someone letting me know he has an appointment in London the day after tomorrow."

"Lovely! We'll take you to dinner!"

"He only has a day and has to be at Heathrow by six."

"Oh. So, you won't see him?"

"He asked whether I'd like to go for a cruise down the Thames."

"Really? So how do you feel about that?"

"Well, I do enjoy boat rides."

EPILOGUE

The islands of the Toronto Island Park were originally a series of sandbars, with currents creating new islands and erasing old ones. There were marshes and shallows between them, and those marshes and shallows could become islands while the islands themselves could be washed away.

The long island was a peninsula until a storm washed away the eastern end, creating an island and a shipping channel. The sands on the south side of Toronto Island shift less noticeably now. A barrier, of rock rather than sand, has been created to the east and prevents the sands from shifting.

There are stories of shipwrecks and death on the south side, in the storms that still go on, but those stories are old. Now the sand on the south side is a series of beaches, which are protected by breakwaters protecting both the beaches and the swimmers. The islands have always been a place of recreation and peace, known to the first people of the area as a sacred place.

The airport has changed but not in major ways. The ferry from the Norwegian barracks has been replaced by a pedestrian tunnel, allowing passengers to walk to the airport easily. The check-in area is small, but the waiting lounge is large, a comfortable place where passengers can sip coffee in soft chairs beside large windows, watching planes nearby, with the Island ferries and sailboats in the background.

***

Flying Through the Ashes

A passenger watching the activity noticed a grey-haired couple walking toward a small plane, the woman carrying a flight kit and the man carrying headphones. When they reached their plane, a Cessna 172, she gave the flight kit to him and surveyed the plane. She checked oil and fuel, examined fuel samples, ran her hands over the forward surfaces of the wings, jiggled the flaps, and pulled out the wheel chocks.

The passenger in the lounge saw conversation between them, with hand gestures toward the sky and the lake. The woman helped the man into the right seat and took the left for herself. The passenger in the lounge wanted to watch more, but his flight was called.

***

In the small plane, the grey-haired couple, Sarah and Ken, buckled their seat harnesses, and then Sarah checked the instruments before turning to Ken.

"It's been a while since you did this. I thought the Niagara tour might be fun."

"Right. Are you ready?"

"Yes. Let's go."

She radioed the tower for permission to taxi for takeoff, took the plane to the runway, and then pushed the throttle forward and pulled back the yoke. The plane rose, and they flew, out over the lake, circling the islands and the beaches before moving up through the layers of air currents, through one with strong force, another with a gentle flow, finally reaching a level of calm, with no challenges beyond the basic requirements of flight.

A FEW WORDS OF THANKS

Any reader will recognize the need for research when writing a book of this nature. There must be errors, which are my own, but I want to thank:

Jan-Terje Studsvik Storaas, of the Royal Norwegian Embassy in Ottawa, Peter Holt, who founded the Toronto Island archives, my friend, Kathryn Shailer, with her deep knowledge of Germany, and my son, Tim, who inspired me to fly.

Thanks, also, to the cheerleaders:

Purabi Sinha Das, who pushed me forward, Ron Thompson, Nancy Kay Clark, Helen Elbertsen, Guy and Carol Kapuscinsky, and my daughter, Elizabeth, who is my cheerleader-in-chief, and who challenges me to move on.